Planet of Muladi

Planet of Muladi

Bella D.

For those who get it.

Acknowledgements

A special thanks to the following people:

My sister Angelina Ding

Raymond Dai
Victor Xu
Chandler Song
Candice Ho
Jenny Yang

for making this book possible.

Bella D.
Instagram @imbe11a

About

There are three stories; there is one story —

The story of our planet;
The story of humanity;
The story of you and me.

Contents

Planet of Muladi

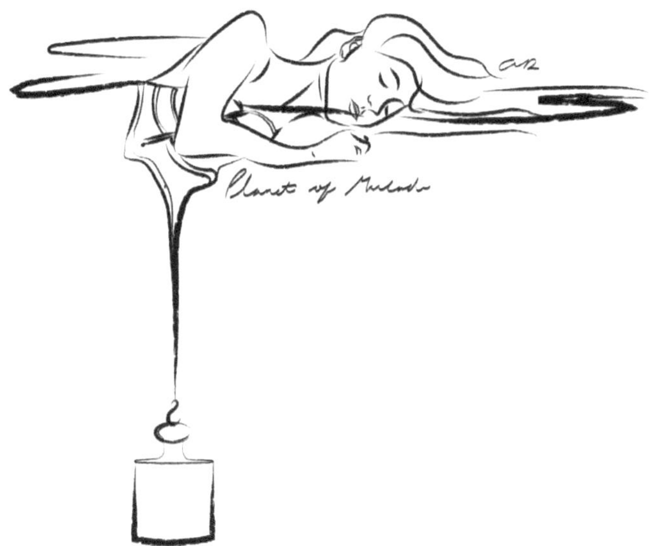

"I've been to the castles of men: those sweeping mansions and towering penthouse suites of allure. They disguise themselves in shining black suits of chivalry, oozing with charm and carefully curated jokes to lure you into their gates. Until you enter their dungeons: they shed their tuxedo plating to reveal the scales they were hiding; their charisma fades into a dry silence. Their castles are museums — with me as their most coveted antique, nurtured for display."

- Planet of Muladi, Chapter 3

1

A fire rages in my skull. In the dark, I instinctively reach toward my bedside table and am met with the sound of shattering ceramics.

I just broke my mother's favorite teacup. Great.

But that's fine. My room is messy enough as it is. Just looks like Jackson Pollock became my interior designer. My fingers reach for the empty pill bottles on my nightstand until they are wrapped around the Tylenol. I gulp down two pills. My body curls inwards like a hedgehog, spikes and all. The temperature of my body is the only thing that adds a sense of security.

Sorry, I forgot to introduce myself. It's not necessary. But if you must know, all you need to know is that I am beautiful. Am I egotistical? No, I'm just honest. Do you hate honesty? Isn't honesty what everyone wants?

"Mu, this project is way beneath you. I realized you have stronger potential in other fields. I have a new assignment. Want to give it a shot?"

"I'd like nothing more!" I burst out excitedly, my heart jumping out of my chest. My first job out of an arduously earned master's degree with the validation from my supervisor (and jealousy from my colleagues) was the best feeling in the world.

God was I naive. Only through the alcohol-drenched stench of men did I realize that I was just one course out of their seven-course feast.

"You are too pretty for an office job," was what he meant.

I don't want to say all this. Sometimes ignorance is bliss. If I am given a second chance, I would love to live a lie.

Hold on a sec. I have a phone call, and there are only two types of people who call me at this hour: those wanting a drink, and those wanting what comes after. Want to take a guess?

"Hey, club tonight? My friend booked the largest booth next to the dance floor."

He just wants an accessory to boost his ego. Men are hypocrites.

"I'm not feeling very well."

"What's wrong?"

"You know, flu season."

"Damn, you ok?"

Of course not.

"I'm fine."

"A drink will make you feel better. There are a lot of people here I can fix you up with. Hot and rich, just how you like it. You sure you don't want to come?"

What, does he think I'm a hypocrite like him?

"Alright. See you in an hour."

Damn right I am.

It's fine. Three more days. I should enjoy myself right?

"Mu, you're the best."

That was what my mother always said.

Yes, Mu, you are the best.

2

Black turtleneck, clean-shaven, hands crossed, eyebrows furrowed. He doesn't belong here. Crap, I think he noticed me. He walks this way and, of course, sits down next to me.

Oh god. Another person who wants to hit on me.

"Hi there."

I muse on my response. I train my eyes forward away from his gaze, pretending not to hear him. Like they say, men like women better when they're deaf and dumb.

"Miss, this may be forward but…"

Go ahead, tell me you find me attractive and want to get to know me. Tell me how fascinating my personality is. Tell me whatever it is you need to get in my pants.

"Your bra is showing."
"Excuse me?"

Oh god, is he a pervert?

"I know I can be a bit direct. Just thought you would want to know."
"Where are you going?"
"Out."

I know what comes next.

"Would you like to come with me?"

What did I tell you? Men are all the same.

"What's your name?"
"Mu."
"What a beautiful name. I am Ladi, Ladi He."

Is that supposed to be a pick-up line? Please excuse me while I gag.

3

I've been to the castles of men: those sweeping mansions and towering penthouse suites of allure. They disguise themselves in shining black suits of chivalry, oozing with charm and carefully curated jokes to lure you into their gates. Until you enter their dungeons: they shed their tuxedo plating to reveal the scales they were hiding; their charisma fades into a dry silence. Their castles are museums — with me as their most coveted antique, nurtured for display.

But Ladi is like no knight I've ever seen. He doesn't offer help to this lady in demounting our steed. His armor was clearly not designer. He does not open my taxi door, nor does our conversation follow any of the pages in Prince Charming's playbook. It is as if he is living in his own mind.

"Wait a minute, where are we going?"

After an hour ride, the taxi turns onto an unmarked, unlit mountain road. Just five minutes of venturing into the darkness, my paranoia sets in. Jesus, he's not a serial killer or a psycho, is he?

"Stop! Taxi, stop!"
"You scared?"

In the darkness, I could've sworn I saw a glimpse of Ted Bundy's smirk. I know what happens next: he would gag me and drug me unconscious. I can already see the China Daily headline: *Attractive Woman's Remains Found In Unmarked Garden.*

"I'm not going to hurt you. We're here."

I look out the window and recoil in surprise. A Guggenheim made of pure glass loomed over the car. Ladi hands the driver a wad of cash as we step out.

What is this, stripper money?

"Let's go."

Three more days before I start my rebellion, and here I am: in front of a strange house with an even stranger man named Ladi.

And I have a feeling that things are going to get stranger.

4

I awkwardly sit in Ladi's cavernous glass dome. Every piece of furniture is immaculately placed, not a cushion out of place. Gold sculptures, gold paintings; what Bond villain did he get as his interior decorator? And who plants a palm tree in the middle of their house?

I whip out my cracked iPhone. Great, of course there's no service on a mountain. Scratching noises materialize behind me. I turn around and I'm greeted by the world's most hideous robot dog.

"This is JoJo, my pet that detects your mood through your body movement."
"You made this?"
"Yes, I'm his creator."

What kind of invention is this? Its appearance is beyond monstrous, like a deformed creature. You'd be hard pressed to sell even one of these on Amazon.

"Wow, how charming! You're a genius!" I flash a smile so fake even Amazon would flag me as false advertising.

"Come."

Finally, here it comes. First, you show off your high tech gadgets. Now it's time for you to seduce me. What's waiting in the bedroom, a high tech bed that detects sexual frequency? I guess we'll have to find out and see.

"What are you waiting for, Mu? Come."

Ladi pulls me into a room with wall-to-wall screens. Just from a quick count, there are probably ten or so screens, each crawling with lines of code. For someone like me who failed computer science, it is all French to me.

Thud. The door shuts heavily.

"What do you want?" There's a terrible feeling in my gut.

"Mu, a Graphic Design graduate from Parsons and currently employed at a small media company in Beijing; promoted to public relations manager half a year ago, reason unstated."

So he's been stalking me? Who in the world is this man? I was promoted because I worked hard!

"You have a private Weibo account where you criticize social issues and satirize your boss and your clients. Ironically, your main account with 523K followers is filled with wholesome pictures and motivational captions."

Jesus, he is a pervert, just not the kind I'm used to dealing with. Is he one of my followers? I must remain calm and rational. I am a lady, after all.

"You are reserved and shut-in but also very arrogant. I can see your on-screen time averages around 8.2 hours a day. You don't have a lot of real friends. Your father passed away when you were ten. Your boyfriend of five years broke up with you before you left New York in 2015."

"Please stop talking."

"You carefully present yourself as the charismatic seductress, yet you can't fully mask your misandrist tendencies. You wrote on your second account: 'All the pieces are in place. Three days and I can take revenge.' Tell me, what are you planning?"

"What do you want from me?"

Did my voice just shake? Sorry, I can't help it.

"I want you to be my first test subject."

"Excuse me?"

Test subject? What am I, his robot dog?

"I haven't thought of a name yet. But since your name is Mu, let's call it Planet Muladi."

Planet Muladi? What does he think he is, *Le Petit Prince?*

Planet of Muladi

5

I lie in my trypophobic inducing massage chair as I quietly mull over all sorts of dreadful thoughts. The scratchy material sends shivers down my spine. I must look like an astronaut, swaddled with thick layers of silver. Ladi is typing quickly on a translucent touch screen. I don't want to disobey him. I'm afraid of what I might see if I refuse.

"Breathe. Don't be nervous."

Why are you telling me this now? Anyone would be nervous lying in a weird massage chair-operating table hybrid.

"Do you know how to put on contact lenses?"
"Of course..."
"Put this on."

Ladi carefully presses a button on a metal box and

gingerly retrieves two pieces of dark grey contact lenses blinking with lines of code.

"You won't go blind. Put them on."

So he's a mind reader now? Wow.

Ladi takes out a translucent remote control with two buttons.

"Press green to enter the planet and red to exit. Whenever you're ready."
"Wait…"
"Yes?"
"How long will the experiment last?"
"Can be a few hours or a few days."
"What if I want to use the toilet?"
"Press the red button."
"Is this life-threatening?"
"No."
"Should I…"
"Why do you have so many questions?"

Fine, I'll shut up. My life is in your hands. Whatever you say, boss.

"Mu."
"Yes?"
"Let me show you a completely new world."

6

To my relief, this experiment is not as surgical as I expected. Thank god there are no needles or blood — I faint when I see blood. I step into a rainbow-colored hole. Swirls of psychedelic colors flash around me. Right as I reach the peak of my unexpected acid trip, I tumble and splash into a pool of slimy liquid. I can feel slime running through my fingers. Above me, a city half submerged in clouds glitters with gold and emerald.

Is this a ripoff of *Alice in Wonderland*?

"Hello, Mu. Welcome to my planet."

That is the voice of Ladi, echoing in the glowing golden sky.

I am bombarded with static noise, like a computer experiencing technical issues. Suddenly, I am teleported into a cottage nestled in ivy. A translucent screen rises from the gilded ground.

"Go pick out your outfit."

I select a minimal, pearl white suit.

"Mu, this is a virtual world."
"So?"
"What is your favorite color?"

When I was young, my favorite Barbie Doll was Rapunzel. I was fascinated by her shimmering violet gown. It was a gift from my father on my tenth birthday.

"Do you like it?"
"I love it! Thank you, papa!"
"Happy birthday, my little princess."
"I'll look so pretty when I wear it to my wedding, with you by my side."
"I can't wait, my darling."

He lied.

"Wow, ten more days before graduation. Time flies, don't you think? Are you still planning on marrying me after?"
"Of course, my princess. You have asked this question already a million times."

Another lie.

I snap back to virtual reality, and realize I am now in

that same violet dress. Nestled between its chiffon folds are clusters of pearls, seashells and lavender glitter. My hair has loosened into golden waves tumbling off my shoulders. A floral scent gently envelopes around me.

"Mu, open your arms."

I gradually raise my arms. In my dream, this scenario has occurred over a hundred times. I flutter into the sky with just a light kick off the ground, breaking free from the gravity that imprisons me in reality.

On the Planet of Muladi, I pass through thousands of small ivy cottages. "Some houses already have residents," Ladi tells me. "And I am the creator."

"Real users living inside?"

"No. They are bots, computer-generated players. There will be real citizens soon."

"A simulated future society? A society ruled by robots?"

"No. It is a society where humans and robots coexist. One day, our planet will be green again. We don't have to immigrate to outer space or live in an underwater city like in those sci-fi films. Technology will change everything and revert earth back to its original glory."

I can't even get my life together. Why should I care about human existence? And even if that day comes, I will be long gone.

"Mu, you must think this has nothing to do with

you."

"I didn't say that. It looks fascinating to me."
"Your expression betrays you."

Oops, I forgot that he's sitting five feet in front of me.

"I understand your skepticism, but you must understand that your problems can be easily resolved if people are no longer bound by the status quo. And status quo is simply a product of inequality."

Is that compassion I sense in his words? Or is it another way for him to satisfy his ego?

"All the cottages are of the same size. On my planet, everyone shares equal rights. There are no poverty gaps or class differences. What matters the most is their self actualization."

During my conversation with Ladi, I can sense his extraordinarily utopian mindset. Perhaps all scientists have this delusion of saving the future. What they forget is that even Einstein ended up creating humanity's greatest weapon of mass destruction.

"So, what is their purpose in life?"
"They're just code. They don't need a purpose."
"I am talking about your future users. I mean, your citizens. What motivates them to play this game?"

Ladi does not answer. His silence makes me a little

nervous. If the program stops, aren't I going to be stuck here forever, living with a bunch of computer-generated bots?

"Ladi, you there?"
"So you think it's only a game."
"No, I meant..."
"We have arrived."

7

In front of me stands a robot. She looks human enough, except her irises are pits of lightless dark pools.

"Welcome, Mu. Now, please choose your favorite occupation."

So I have to work?

"Designer, I guess."

"According to your spike in brainwave activity and increased heart rate, this answer has a 90% chance of being a lie. Please follow your heart and choose again."

Did he implant some sort of lie detection program in me?

"Well, I studied graphic design, and I do really like this job."

"Humans tend to hide their real motives and thoughts. According to a study conducted in 1977 at Villanova and Temple Universities, the illusory truth effect states that humans begin to believe a piece of information after being falsely repeated over and over to them. The illusory truth effect plays a significant role in election campaigns, advertising, and propaganda. However, your brain and heart rate do not lie, Mu. Therefore, please pick another career."

"Fine, fine. I've always wanted to live on a mountain with a horse and a small art studio. I can draw whatever I want, whenever I want, not having to modify them into some shit looking commercial piece to please my boss. I won't have to work like a robot, doing the same thing every day like you. Ok but you know what, this is a bit too unrealistic. Sorry, let me think of something else…"

Wait, why am I apologizing to a robot in a virtual world? I must be insane.

"According to your brain waves and heart rate, this answer has a 95% accuracy rate. We will arrange the most suitable career for you. On the Planet of Muladi, we make everything possible. We are committed to providing our residents with the best lifestyle. Now, please place your right hand onto this screen."

"Congratulations, Mu. You are officially the first resident of Planet of Muladi!"

"Ladi, you there?"

"I'm here," his voice comes from far away.

"So I need to earn money in a game?"

"Working allows you to be self-sufficient, Mu. As long as you do what you love, you will earn Ladicoins every day. In the future, every citizen will earn the same salary."

Ladicoins? What kind of Bitcoin bullshit is this? Earning the same salary while pursuing what you love sounds like a fantasy — but just that: a fantasy.

"Sorry to break it to you Ladi, Communism doesn't work, just look at what happened to...."

I really can't help myself anymore.

"Elaborate."

"You see, if your game enters the market, people need some incentive to play it, right? If there is no class difference or challenge to overcome, they will get bored easily."

"That's not the reason I created this world."

"Then why?"

"To elevate human happiness levels, Mu. To help people find themselves again."

"How do you define 'happiness levels'? So are you gonna make every player lie in your weird massage chairs and swaddle them in aluminum foil? We're humans, not baked goods."

And furthermore, "help people find themselves"? Does he think he's god?

"These aren't things you should worry about."
"I need to use the toilet!"

And oh how tiring this whole ordeal has been. I know it is daytime in the game, but I'm already half asleep.

"Press the red button and exit the game."

I see a mass of codes crashing down and hear a piercing noise that lasts for five seconds. "Ladi, I nearly went blind! And deaf!"

"Program error. Let me take this off for you."

God damn it, my ears are still ringing. It feels a hundred times worse than a long night of clubbing.

"You can rest here tonight."

I suppose that was rather long when it comes to foreplay, and I am definitely not turned on.

"What I mean is, you will sleep in the guest room. There are new toiletries in the bathroom. Rest well."

It looks like he had already prepared everything beforehand. Jesus, I'm going to be stuck here forever aren't I?

"Goodnight, Mu."

Half an hour later, I fall into a deep sleep.

8

Ladi must be the wealthiest person I've ever met. Excluding the insane amount his tech equipment must cost, even his breakfast plates calculate calories and utensils beep when you're eating too fast. Even if I were able to become that rich, I would never want to live in such a systemized house like this. It would drive me crazy.

"Ladi, what's your horoscope?"
"Virgo, why?"

Well, that explains a lot.

"You?"
"Didn't you already investigate me thoroughly?"
"I don't look into horoscopes."
"Then how come you know yours?"
"My ex-girlfriend told me."

Wow, tech Jesus had a girlfriend? I assumed he makes

love to robots.

"Are you ready?"
"I have a question."
"Another one?"
"As your lab rat, don't I get paid?"

Come on, show me some sincerity.

"Wait for me in the room once you are ready."

Fine. He knows nothing about social etiquette. Despite all my complaints, I am actually somewhat looking forward to what's coming next. To have such a strange experience two days before I start my rebellion is pretty cool.

"Ladi what's your Wifi password?"

I'm not trying to escape or send for help. It's just that the last twelve hours without the internet has felt like a century.

"Why?"
"Just want to call my mom on Wechat, that's all."

I want to let her know that I am safe. I didn't come home last night. I hope she hasn't called the police.

"Sure."

Guess he's not so bad after all.

"Hello, who's there?"
"Mama, it's me."
"Mu? You changed your number?"

Of course she didn't notice.

"Mama, where are you? It's so loud on your end."
"I flew to Dali yesterday! Didn't I tell you? I got a new boyfriend, and we are going away for three days! He's the VP of some large Fortune 500, Mu!"
"What company, mama?"
"I forgot, but he does have a Ferrari!"
"Oh."
"When I return home, I'll take you two for lunch, and you can meet him!"
"Alright. Have fun, mama."
"Ok, I'm gonna go now! He booked a Michelin restaurant for dinner. Honey, I'm coming! Yes, Mu just called me…"

With that, I'm greeted with the sound of the phone clicking again.

"Shall we begin?"

I take a deep breath and press the green button.

9

I hear a chorus of crickets singing. There it is, a golden mare tied under a lemon tree. Not far away beyond a picket fence stands that ivy entwined cottage.

"Welcome back, Mu. This cottage was made based on your description. Are you satisfied?"

"Very much, thank you."

"Great to hear that, Mu. The Planet of Muladi strives to provide the most comfortable and ideal living environment for all our citizens. On behalf of the planet's government, I wish you a pleasant stay!"

"Government? Who's the leader? Ladi?"

"The government of Muladi is artificial intelligence like me. We make the most humane decisions for our citizens based on precise calculations."

"How are you supposed to know what 'humane' is if you're not even human?"

"That is a good question, Mu. Have you heard of the Seven Deadly Sins?"

"Nope."

"No worries, Mu. I will explain it to you. The Seven Deadly Sins include pride, greed, lust, envy, gluttony, wrath, and sloth. The desire for wealth and the battle for power will one day deplete your Earth of resources, with humanity paying a terrible price. Our existence is to save humanity because we are designed to make the most comprehensive and impartial decisions based on advanced algorithms. Does this answer your question, Mu?"

Did tech Jesus write that script? Makes me wanna puke.

"Tell me, how do you plan to save us?"

"Apologies, Mu. That is out of my cognitive range."

"Nevermind. You can leave now."

"Alright, Mu. Planet of Muladi strives to provide the most comfortable and ideological living environment for our citizens. On behalf of our government, I wish you a pleasant stay!"

On the screen materializes a holographic city map that directs me to open the resident manual on the bottom right corner.

"Congratulations Mu! You are the first official resident of Muladi. Planet of Muladi exists to increase the happiness of our citizens. To improve our society, we wish for you to contribute to our economy. As long as you complete three tasks every day, you will earn the day's Ladicoin."

"Can you hear me, Mu?" Ladi's voice echoes throughout the room. "Select your top three tasks. As of today, the game already consists of over a hundred different options. There must be one that you like. Keep this in mind: the system will prompt you to pick again if you select dishonestly."

"What if I don't do any task at all?"

"Then you won't be able to earn today's Ladicoins."

"What are they for?"

"If you want to enjoy other leisure activities like buying new clothes or doing your hair, you will need your Ladicoins."

In the next few hours, I swiftly explore the planet riding my golden mare. I venture into the forest for a horse-riding lesson with a robot that looks exactly like young Brad Pitt. If I don't constantly remind myself that he's fake, I'd absolutely love to have a different kind of riding lesson.

After my equestrian adventure, I visit a racecourse and choose the most expensive-looking race car. I do not know how to drive in real life. In fact, I don't need to drive. As long as I wag my little pinkie finger, men will race to my side, chauffeur-ready. However, in this world, I surprisingly land second place in the race track.

"Congratulations on completing your first race with the HEV Laslas No.100. Next, you shall complete your final task of the day. What would you like to choose?"

"I want to go back to my cottage and paint."

"Alright, Mu. I will now…"

The robot's voice is suddenly interrupted by a piercing screech. The planet disintegrates into a swarm of static. After a few seconds, Muladi becomes dead silent.

"Ladi? I want to go home!"

No reply. Perhaps he went to the washroom?

"Ladi! Are you there?"

I shakily feel around for the transparent remote control and quickly press down the red button. I close my eyes, bracing myself for that piercing noise. However, the world remains silent.

I furiously stab the red button repeatedly, shrieking Ladi's name. What should I do? Just take off the helmet? Will I be electrified to death? Continue waiting? What if something happened to him? If I am stuck here forever, at least give me some damn Wifi.

Hold on, why do I fear of death?

"Mu, can you hear me?"
"Ladi! Jesus, you scared me to death! Where did you go?"
"I went to take a call."
"I want to go home."
"Discontinue the experiment?"

"I meant back to the cottage. Don't I have to complete one more task?"

"Oh. Sure."

"One more thing, I wanted to exit the game earlier but could not. Why is that?"

"That's not possible. You should exit once you press the red button. Can you try again?"

I press the red button again. I'm greeted once more with the deafening silence.

"That's not possible."

10

I'm huddled up on a deadly silent race track. Each moment feels like an eternity.

"Try to stay calm. Let me check where the error was. Talk to me."

"I have nothing to say to you." I burst out furiously.

"How was it?"

It was great. The past hour had almost made me forget all of my frustrations. I felt like Tinkerbell released back into Neverland.

"The system is rebooting."

"So do you believe that technology will turn the world into a better place?"

"I do."

"But does your belief matter? The robot was right. Humans are inherently selfish and full of sin. As long as humans exist, we will always exist for ourselves. There is no Mother Theresa who will sacrifice themselves for a greater cause."

"Sacrifice? If one day artificial intelligence can perform all the tasks to fulfill our basic material needs, then humans like you will have the opportunity to explore your potential and do what you truly love. Mu, do you think you're sacrificing something playing this game? Tell me Mu, are you happy?"

"Mu, are you happy?"
"Of course I'm happy. I'm with you."
"But I'm not happy, Mu."
"Why?"
"I haven't figured out what I want yet. I don't see a future with you."
"So what do you want? Weren't we always good together? What kind of future are we looking at?"
"I don't know and I feel lost. You're right. Everything is perfectly fine right now. But I don't know what I want in my future. I need some time to figure it all out."
"Can't we figure it out together?"
"I'm sorry I've made up my mind. I wish you all the best."

"Mu, the reboot is at 90% completion. In a few seconds, you will hear the sharp noise like you did yesterday. Hey, are you ok? You look a bit pale. Mu? Mu?"

I don't remember what happens next, only a stifling heaviness; a pair of warm hands holding my head; a stern voice repeating my name, over and over again.

All I want is to feel this heavy forever, and fall into a deep, deep sleep.

11

I see myself tumbling down a hole. Once again, I land in Muladi. However, the greenery has dulled into a lifeless brown. I am drowned in the stench of rust and gasoline — the scent of swarms of robots as they trample over my naked body. The wall of lightless, crescent-shaped eyes smirk at me, muttering in a language I cannot understand.

"Jesus, what happened here?"
"Welcome back, Mu."
"What is all this..."
"This is what the planet looks like 500 years from now."
"What? But..."
"Don't you understand, Mu? Humans are selfish and full of sin. They are our god and created a new civilization by destroying their old one. Therefore, we will continue your legacy and guard your world for the generations to come."

"I don't understand. Didn't Ladi say that everything will return to its most primal state?"

"Mu, have you heard of the famous Murphy's Law? Edward Murphy's law can be understood as the equation pn=1-(1-p)n. You look lost. Let me explain it to you. If there are two methods for something, one of the options would likely lead to disaster. Therefore, there must be someone who would make this choice. Do you understand?"

"I don't..."

"Here's another way to explain this. If something can go wrong, no matter how small the possibility it is, it will always happen. Do you understand?"

"No, I don't understand!"

"If you are worried about something, it is more likely to happen. Do you understand?"

"Shut up already! I don't fucking understand! What makes you think you can teach me a lesson? Everything you say is programmed by humans. You are nothing more than our tool! A tool! Do *you* understand?"

My cries are like dying animals in their death throes, only to be drowned out by lifeless, metallic laughter.

"You are very emotional at this moment, Mu. Your heartbeat is fluctuating rapidly, which is life-threatening. I would suggest that you remain calm. Would you like me to recommend some methods for calming yourself?"

"No, I don't need your help, okay? What are you doing? Let go of me! Let go of me *now*!"

Robot Brad Pitt approaches me, lifts me with one hand, and throws me into a rusting cage visibly marked with animal scratches. I see wisps of brown hair. Thousands of robots surround me and sneer through their metal teeth, bombarding me with coins and banana peels. I shut my eyes, refusing to face this atrocity. I opened my eyes and my cage has multiplied, now each holding my mom, my boss, my colleagues, and hundreds of other familiar faces.

"Why did you do this to us, Mu! Your ignorance will kill us all!"

The red button. Where is the red button? I have to press the red button. A fire sears through my brain until it burns out my vision and I'm left frozen in the dark. I want to scream, but no sound comes out. I force my eyes open and I see Ladi sitting by my bed, his concerned gaze trained onto me. I rub my tear-soaked eyes. Oh god, only the devil knows what I just experienced.

So was that just a nightmare?

"You're finally awake."
"How long was I out?"
"It's already 8 pm. You have a fever, Mu. Sit up and take a Tylenol."

Why am I sick?

"You're stressed and anxious, not to mention probably suffering the side effects of the experiment. Today you must rest. We have one more day to go."

"I had a terrible nightmare, Ladi."

"I know. You were screaming."

"And you didn't wake me up?"

"You'll wake up when you want to wake up."

"Ladi?"

"Yes?"

"Tell me, what does the future look like?"

"That's hard for me to answer."

"Tell me please."

Ladi falls silent for a few seconds. He turns to leave, then pauses. With his back towards me, he gingerly responds.

"The future is whatever you choose to believe."

12

Eighteen hours before my rebellion and Ladi has powered up yet another lab chair. It's dark. Inside this ethereal space, I see thousands of blinking green lights.

"What the hell is this place?"
"You're half right."
"Don't tell me this is a haunted house. I hate haunted houses."

"Greetings Ms. Mu and Mr. Ladi. I am Morse, your administrator. Welcome to Muladi activity No. 0113: The Near-Death Experience Lab."
"Ladi, that's another robot right?"

Jesus, am I out of my mind? What else could it be, a human? Though I must admit that in the past few days, the line between reality and fantasy has blurred to the point where I have to question my sanity every couple seconds. This "experiment" seems to have infected my consciousness. It has permeated my veins, my cells, my bloodstream, and my very soul, leaving me questioning the nature of reality.

Is this what the future looks like?

"As the administrator of the Near-Death Experience Lab, my job is to actualize the experience of death. After this experience, we hope that our residents will acquire a deeper understanding of death. Do you have any questions, Ms. Mu?"
"No... Nope."
"Alright, Ms.Mu. Let us begin."

13

"Every green light you see here is an active nerve cell from your brain. They may be a memory, a plan, or someone you miss. Would you like to see what your brain is thinking right now, Ms. Mu?"

"You can do that?"

"Of course. Please select a green particle."

I reach out with my right hand and grab the nearest green light . I am instantly transported back to that 3 ½ New York apartment. I see my knock-off Supreme-wearing younger self, standing amidst a littered living room.

"You like influencers that much? You would toss away five years for an influencer?"

"How many times do you need me to spell it out for you? It's not because of her. It's because I don't see a future with you!"

"Liar! It's just because of her! What's good about her? Just because I'm not part of that social media circle

and she has more followers than me? We've been together for *five years*! Give me back my five years!"

"Calm down, Mu! I'll say it one last time. Our break-
up has nothing to do with her."

"You asshole! I want you out of my house! You will
regret this! You and that plastic surgery whore deserve
each other. I wish you two are happy together. *Happily.
Ever. After!*"

I grabbed the cushion on the sofa and threw it at the
retreating figure. The door slammed shut, rattling the
floorboards.

"Mu, now please select a different particle."

The next scene appears as a blur. I blink my eyes to focus
and strain my ears to hear, only to make out faint ap-
plause, soft reverberations of footsteps, and outlines of
shadowy figures.

"What am I seeing?"

"This is your brain's prediction of the future. I cannot decipher what this entails from our statistics. Perhaps
only you can understand. Now, please select another."

"Why are you doing this, mama? Can you even live
by yourself?"

"My sweet daughter. We must always look forward."

"You never loved my father! You only loved his money!"

"Is that any way to talk to your mother? If only your

father could hear the filth coming out of your mouth! He would be appalled!"

"You don't deserve to be called my mother. I'm cutting you out; I have no mother!"

"Go ahead. Aggravate your mother to death, is that what you want? I'll tell you this. From now on, do whatever you want, I don't care."

My mother's eyes seemed to crease with more wrinkles. This was just one of our countless arguments. But after I plotted my rebellion, I stopped caring enough to argue.

"Ms. Mu, usually when one is consumed by suicidal thoughts, they don't want to kill themselves, but rather kill their current lifestyle. The first light particle you selected represents the past you do not wish to confront and the lifestyle it has prompted you to engage in.

"The second light particle is a representation of the future your brain longs for and what you hope to accomplish. The last light particle represents a problem in your current life. Now, we will proceed to the second phase of our experiment. Are you ready?"

14

"Wait. This won't hurt, will it?"
"Not to worry, Ms. Mu."
"Alright. I'm ready."
"Please lie down."

Suddenly I feel two bursts of energy cleave through me. It feels like my body is being torn apart apart as I begin drifting upwards, yet my body very clearly is still on the table. A channel of light showers me from above. A fluorescent halo lights up my corporeal body lying on the translucent table. My soul rises up into the dazzling tunnel of light. I see my father on the other side. He's exactly as I remember him; crisp white shirt paired with his tender smile.

"Why are you here, my little princess? This is not where you're meant to be."
"Take me with you papa. You're the only person in this world who cares about me."

"Sweetheart. Do you remember what you promised me when you were ten?"

"I remember, but…"

"Take care of your mother. Take care of your home. I'm gone and your mother is getting old. You have to be the caretaker of our family now. You must learn to be strong; learn to endure; and learn to forgive. Can you promise me that sweetheart?"

"Ms. Mu, can you hear me? How are you feeling right now?"

Morse's voice sucks my consciousness back into my body. I awaken, lost in a pool of despair. The green specks grow more and more distant until I am engulfed in darkness. When I blink again, I feel tears rolling down my cheeks.

"Morse, what's the meaning of life?"

I have to ask.

"To pursue happiness, Ms. Mu. Humans exist to pursue their happiest, most becoming lifestyle. Perhaps you will suffer, perhaps you will cry, perhaps you will feel unloved during your pursuit. However, one day, you will find your purpose and attain the life you always wanted. One day, the world will become what it once was: a green planet just like Muladi, filled with love and happiness."

"I doubt I'll live long enough to see that ideal world."

"Ms. Mu. The future is whatever you choose to believe. Right, Mr. Ladi?"

Ladi does not reply. He presses down the red button on his remote.

"Our experiment has finished. You can go home now, Mu."

"Ladi?"

"Yes?"

"Will we see each other again?"

"I don't think so."

Ladi opens the holographic glass gate. His hideous robot dog wags his tail at me, nuzzling against my leg.

"Ladi?"

"Yes?"

"It was great to meet you. Goodbye."

"Goodbye, Mu."

15

On the rooftop of a particular skyscraper located in downtown Beijing, a girl stands shivering in the freezing wind. That's right, that girl is me. How did I get up there? Of course, it's thanks to my ability to seduce men; in particular the security guard at the reception. You know how this goes: I'm Mu. No man can resist me.

I am the beautiful Mu. You should congratulate me. We have finally reached the day of my rebellion. On the same day it starts it will end.

The building is 500 meters high. If Newton's Law holds up, I'll fall at about 55 meters per second. Before I splatter into a pile of dirt, I'll experience 9 seconds of free fall. A white sheet will cover my body. Maybe I'll make the news. "Inspirational Lifestyle Blogger Dead From Apparent Suicide," the headline will read. My diehard followers may mourn my death for a few days before forgetting about my existence entirely.

"It's a shame she didn't think it through," some may say. "She was such a pretty and inspiring role model."

Days later, I will be forgotten. My father once told me that the most precious gems last the shortest, and therefore, we must treasure them the most. But now, I understand. Gems have an expiration date because they're just meteorites: falling stars disintegrating in an ephemeral spectacle all for our viewing pleasure. But it's never enough. And soon enough, like everything else, gems will be crushed by time's unrelenting fingers back into dust, drifting aimlessly through space and time. Dust to dust, ashes to ashes.

Am I right? I must be right.

"Mu, the future is whatever you choose to believe."

I hear Ladi's voice next to me.

"Ladi, is that you? Tell me, what should I do?"

Silence.

"Mu?"
"Ladi?"
"When you were on Muladi, were you happy?"
"Yes. I was happy. But I can't look back. I can't go back, Ladi."

I remember the golden green shimmer of Muladi and

my ivy cottage. I don't think I actually opened my art studio. I don't think I had the chance to explore my potential. I'll miss the Planet of Muladi being introduced to our real world, being praised by millions.

"Ladi, tell me. Tell me!"

Rain starts to trickle down Beijing's night sky. Gently at first, then beating against my violet Dior slip dress. Jesus, I don't want my beautiful corpse to turn out like a drowned rat.

"Mu, trust me."
"Trust you on what?"
"You know what."

I know what Ladi wants to say, but everything has been decided.

"I didn't get to say this yesterday. Thank you, Ladi."
"You have to trust me."
"I'm sorry. I've made up my mind."
"The future is whatever you choose to believe."

The future is whatever you choose to believe.

- *FIN* -

Nerissa

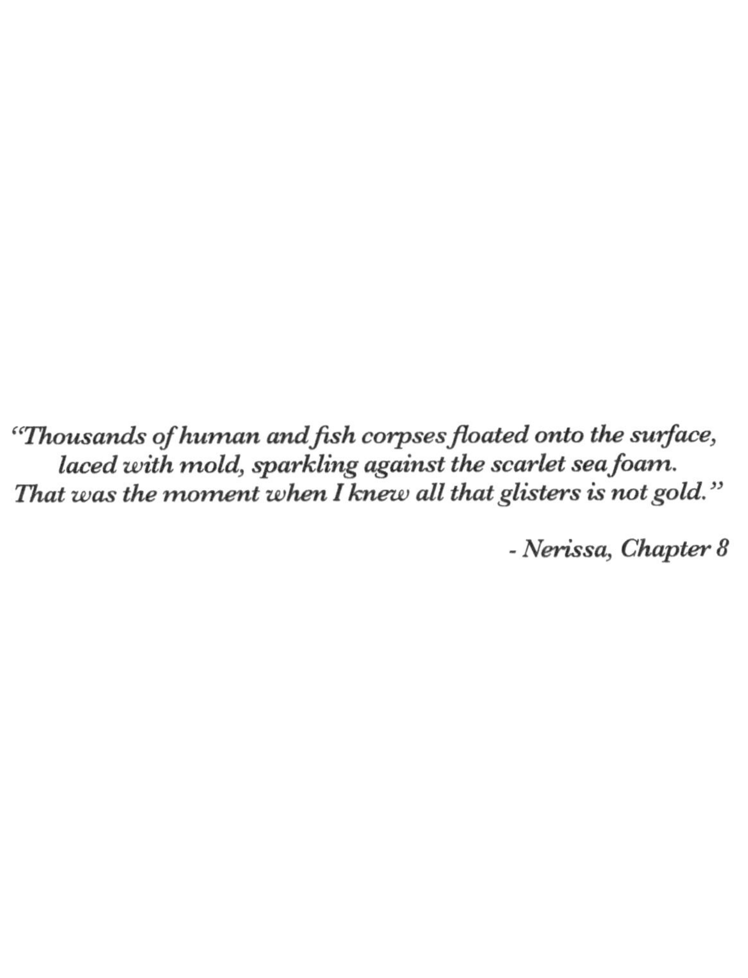

*"Thousands of human and fish corpses floated onto the surface,
laced with mold, sparkling against the scarlet sea foam.
That was the moment when I knew all that glisters is not gold."*

- Nerissa, Chapter 8

1

My name is Nerissa, a first-generation mermaid. My story starts at the age of sixteen. Before sixteen, I lived in a little glass box. Anna always told me I was a child of the gods.

"Your birth is a miracle. You're a huge leap for mankind."

"What is mankind?"

"Gods who created your body and mind."

Anna told me that I would receive a birthday gift when I turned sixteen, something I've always dreamed of.

"What is a birthday gift?"

"A birthday gift celebrates you turning a year older."

"How come I've never gotten birthday gifts before?"

"Because sixteen will be a memorable year. Where I come from, sixteen means you're half a grown-up."

"Where did you come from, Anna?"

"I came from…" Anna hesitated, then smiled at me, "a land far far away."

Anna loved telling me stories. She told me tales of a little town filled with sunlight. Every morning, tree leaves would sprinkle dewdrops into her grandmother's glass jar of pink petals. She would turn them into rose tea for her and her brother to drink.

"What is sunlight?"

"Sunlight is the light that comes from the sun. The sun is a star that warms the world. For many years, this star has given us light and life."

"I wish I was like you. I've never seen sunlight before."

"Silly girl, you don't need sunlight. You are Nerissa, the daughter of the sea. The water and waves are what you are meant to need."

I was always curious about why Anna looked different from me. Why were Anna's hands long and graceful but mine wide and clumsy? Why did Anna turn her head to see, but for me, there was no need?

"Do you miss your brother, Anna?"

"Of course, and my grandmother too. They are my family. I love them very much. Do you know what love is, Nerissa?"

"Love? What's love?"

Anna blinked her emerald green eyes, "You will understand when you turn sixteen."

Finally, the big day had come. I could not sleep the whole night, thinking of what surprise was there awaiting. But that morning, it was not Anna who came to see me.

"Hello, you must be Nerissa."
"Who are you? Where is Anna?"
"Anna? She fell asleep."
"When will she wake up?"
"She might never wake up. Just pretend that she went away."
"Where did she go? Back to the town of sunlight and rose tea?"
"What town? My dear, where can you find sunlight and rose tea in this world you see?"
"Isn't it the town where she grew up in? Anna told me that's where her brother and grandma will be."
"Silly dear, Anna's brother and grandma are gone. But no worries, my child, I'll now open your water tank, and you can move along."

For the first time in sixteen years, I was leaving. I blew bubbles as butterflies fluttered in my belly.

"Go on, my dear. The world is now yours."

I am Nerissa, a first-generation mermaid. On my sixteenth birthday, Anna said there would be a surprise waiting for me.

"My dear, tomorrow is the big day."

"Yes! But why do you look so grey?"

"Just a bit tired. Remember my words. When you go out into the world, learn to love. Love mankind: they are your god. Love your own: they are your peers. Love the ocean: it is your home. And most of all, love every living creature in the sea. You live in karma's world; you can't escape it. Treat others the way you want to be treated. Protect this deep blue and every creature that lives around you. Do you understand?"

"Yes, Anna. Although I only half know what you mean, I promise to remember what you told me."

"Good girl. Now, go to sleep."

"I will. Goodnight, Anna."

"Goodnight. Goodbye, Nerissa."

2

When I lived in my little glass cube, Anna tossed goodies into my feeding tube. My favorite was shrimp wrapped with seaweed that I could gulp down more than fifty. Anna always worried that I would be overweight, "You gained weight again, Nerissa, only twenty shrimps this time."

"Oh, Anna, don't be selfish!"

"Fine, twenty-one, now don't you whine."

After I got out of my little glass cube, the first thing I noticed was that there were more kinds of food than what Anna was putting in my feeding tube. I opened my mouth in a giant O to gulp down a whole of flat yellow fish. How delicious! Anna told me to love every living creature in the sea, so I'll just eat one, just one only.

"Don't eat this, silly. You'll chip your teeth."

"And who in the sea will you be?"

"So you are Nerissa? The mermaid newly released?"

On the day of my sixteenth birthday, I met someone that looked exactly like me: a streamlined body and skin bright and shiny; no hair on his head and eyes that spin all around. But his tail was dark blue when mine was lavender, and he was also much stronger than me; probably ate one shrimp too many.

"So who in this sea would you be?"
"Call me Lynn."
"Is it also your birthday today?"
"No. I am already eighteen, little girl."
"So what were you doing when you turned sixteen and seventeen?"
"Waiting for you."
"Waiting for me?"
"Yes. Waiting for you, Nerissa."
"Alright then. Now hurry up and show me the outside world!"

On the day of my sixteenth birthday, the second thing I learned was how fast I could swim. When I was kept in my little glass cube, all I would do was wag my tail and count my scales. Anna once said that a new row of scales would grow as I turned a year older. That day, I counted sixteen rows from my waist to my tail.

Lynn guided me through a school of little fish. As we approached another glass cube, I started to grow anxious.

"Oh no, are you locking me up once more?"
"Why do you think that? No Nerissa, come with me.

Isn't the outside world what you want to see? Come here and take a peek at this crystal ball. What are you doing? Why are you reaching out your hand? This is only a projection, don't you understand? It's fake; you won't feel anything."

"What? What is it?"

"This is a computer, Nerissa. It's our window to the outside world."

"Aren't we in the outside world?"

"The outside world is mankind's world. But don't venture out of this space. Mankind's world is a dangerous place."

"You're lying Lynn. I know of mankind's world. It is a world of sunlight and rose tea. Anna already told me."

"Silly girl, we don't need sunlight. The heat burns us, and we will die."

"Die? What do you mean die?"

"Death is when you leave this world forever after closing your eyes."

"So if I close my eyes right now will I die?"

"No, are you dumb? Silly girl, of course not."

Anna never told me what death was. At age sixteen, I did not understand it at all. Only when I saw the thousands of bodies floating on the sea did I know the true meaning of war, death, and tragedy.

After that day, Lynn and I explored our surroundings, with people coming to check on us every other week. Lynn and I made up some new recipes. I loved to swallow sea stars wrapped in seaweed. The slick and slippery seaweed wrapping the thick and sticky star skin was just too delicious not to eat! From time to time, I felt our ocean rumble and tremble slightly.

"It had always been this way," Lynn told me, "probably just another earthquake, the Earth's way to stretch."

My favorite place to visit was the crystal ball in my glass treasure chest, where I met fluffy pandas and vicious leopards — and many other creatures who roamed on the ground.

"Hello crystal ball, I'm back!"

"Hello, Nerissa. What would you like to see today?"

"Show me some movies that humans like to watch."

"Okay, not a problem. According to your interests, I've selected the genres sci-fi, comedy, and romance. Which would you prefer?"

"What in the sea are you watching? Turn it off! Crystal ball, go to sleep!"

"What's wrong, Lynn?"

"Are you a fool Nerissa? You're still a kid, how can you watch pornography?"

"But Anna told me that I have to learn how to love! And why are you always so mean, calling me a fool? That is so rude!"

"Learning how to love is not learning how to *make* love, fool. From now on, you must do some proper learning. Go on and finish the human encyclopedia, that will teach you the right things."

"Fine, you meanie. And you should learn too; learn

how to be nice to a lady."

"Do what I say and shut up already."

Lynn told me that the most exceptional talent of mermaids was our photographic memory. Indeed, I had learned thirty languages in less than a year. My favorite was French. The hardest was Chinese. I could never understand why the Chinese created so many complicated characters. However, after a year of studying, I had a good grasp on all of them.

"By the end of the 22nd century, 96% of the Earth's Arctic glaciers had melted. The Earth's population had reached 10 billion. The United States, China, and Central South Asia had built ten cities atop oceans. 32.5% of the sea had become severely polluted, and scientists from 30 countries around the world began building the most abundant marine sanctuary in Monaco.

"By the start of the 23rd century, humans had still not yet located a suitable planet for immigration. However, they had successfully completed the world's first underwater city, Milana. This city, isolated from the outside world in the Ligurian Sea, cost a total of 10 billion US dollars. It now houses select residents from around the world, along with 862 endangered marine species."

"In the late 23rd century, Dutch scientist Edward Joseph and his AI team announced the revolutionary invention of the first mermaid species who could live deep under the sea. Look, Lynn, that's us! Look at this!

Mermaids are not considered to be mammals but as a species of fish. However, their neural systems are a hundred times stronger than humans. Edward believes that mermaids could help humanity create a marine civilization and dominate the ocean. Lynn, don't you think this encyclopedia is a bit strange?"

"Why is that?"

"Look here… the chapters from the year 2249 to 2299 are inaccessible. It says that they require 'the administrator's password'. Lynn, what do you think happened in these 50 years?"

"Might just be some humanity's darkest secrets."

"What are 'secrets'?"

"Secrets are the things that humans don't want us fish to know."

During my sixteenth year, I met some new friends, including a sea turtle I named Annie, who always tailed behind us. Annie looked a little different from the turtles I saw in the crystal ball. Her skin was hard as a stone. Was she afraid I was going to eat her?

"Anna disappeared so now it's just you and me. Isn't that right, Annie?"

When I got tired of swimming, I sat on Annie's shiny shell. Lynn always called me lazy. His favorite hobby was to tone his body using the *Mermaid Fitness Guide* he found in the crystal ball. Day after day, Lynn, Annie and I would play. I used to believe that, all my life, it would just be Lynn, Annie, and I. But on my seventeenth birthday, everything changed.

When I woke up to prepare myself a giant lobster meal, Lynn pulled me aside.

"What are you doing? Hey, slow down! I can't swim as fast as you!"

"Come with me. I've discovered a huge secret."

"What is it? Did you prepare a birthday gift?"

"Exactly, a birthday surprise. Swim faster, you lazy girl. Told you you should've worked out with me."

"Where are we going? Where is this place?"

"The border between us and the outside world."

3

"Why are we here, Lynn? I'm starving."

"Wanna search for food outside?"

"I don't think…"

"You scaredy-cat!"

"You're the brave one, go by yourself! Besides, it's locked! We can't get out."

"Easy," Lynn rolled his eyes mysteriously. "Haven't you noticed? Whenever a human comes for our body checks, he has a belt of fifty numbers and twenty-six letters wrapped around his waist. That is the code to the door. I've seen them exit that way with my very own eyes. Even more, that lock not only has an electronic identification system but also a manual override. Nerissa, today is your birthday. They definitely will come and wish you a happy birthday. Just act as if your tail hurts and bend down. Then, all you've got to do is remember the password."

"But Lynn! I don't think this is right."

"Weren't you curious about what happened in the

last fifty years? Maybe we'll find some answers in the human world."

"But you also told me then that the human world is dangerous!"

"Don't you want to know? Tell me, Nerissa, do you want to be locked up in this cage for the rest of your life?"

Lynn's question got to me. He really knew how to persuade me. You must think I was a hypocrite. Even though I did not approve of his plan, I went ahead with it anyway. I followed Lynn's instructions and successfully caught sight of the fifty digit password. I clutched his hand as we swam back to the so-called border of our world. This time, I did not just peer at it from a distance, but tiptoed towards it.

"Oh my, so we are really still living in a big glass cage!"

I could not really see what was out there. That frightened me. I pressed my face on the glass and rolled my eyes all around, straining to see the distance. But all I could see was a sea of darkness.

"Lynn, I think we should still not do it."

"You scaredy-cat. Then just tell me the password, and I'll go myself."

"Ok fine. Where do I enter the password? Here?"

"Wait, don't do it just yet. You see the light blinking up there?" Lynn lowered his voice. "I saw it in one of the crystal ball's movies — that is a surveillance camera. Which means that humans can see every move we make. We must first swim over there block it with seaweed tape."

I started to admire Lynn. Even though he had told me that we mermaids have higher intelligence than human beings, I was still frustrated. Just two years older than me, Lynn always thought one step ahead, one level more nuanced. So there is an IQ difference within our own fish species?

Following Lynn's directions, we surprisingly unlocked the complex jumble of codes easily and swam out the gate. It was almost like fate, how smoothly this day had been going. Lynn heaved open the heavy glass door. I realized that it was not the glass that was black, but rather the outside world itself.

Darkness, the sea was a pool of darkness.

"Ly… Lynn. Are you sure about this?"
"Stay there and don't move. Wait for me."
"Where are you going?"
"I'm gonna scout the area first."
"No, I will go with you."

"Hey Lynn, you see the dot of light? Is that the sun?"

After my eyes adjusted to the darkness, Lynn pulled me forwards, swimming upwards towards the only light. As we got closer, I realized that the dot was not light, but a city! A city submerged within the ocean!

"Milana? Lynn, is this the marine city?"

"Shh, lower your voice. Yes, I believe there is no other marine city."

"But it looks different from what I saw in the photos. Are you sure we should enter? Wait, wait for me!"

I saw many pictures of Milana inside the crystal ball. According to the encyclopedia, humans and fish coexisted happily in the city. However, since we arrived here, I had not seen a single fish. The only surprising thing was the multiple giant crystal balls, lighting up each building with a faint beam of light.

"Lynn, I really am hungry."

"Let's go search for some food."

We took a lap around the city, then finally found what looked like grocery store nestled in one of the spheres. We circled the store, trying to find an entrance.

"Lynn, we are fish. Anna told me that humans need air to breathe, but we do not. I want to enter, but how? We should go home now. They must be worried that we've disappeared for so long."

"Who's there?"

A deep voice echoed from above me, scaring me.

"Who's there? Answer or I'll shoot."

"Hello sir, I am Lynn. This is Nerissa. We are the first-generation mermaids."

"Mermaids?"

An old man with silvery hair stepped out of the grocery store and slowly approached us. His jaw dropped.

"You two are mermaids? Mermaids exist?"

"Yes, sir."

"So you two are invented by Edward?"

"Yes, sir. You know Edward, our god?"

"Then have you seen my sister Anna?"

"Anna? Anna is your sister? But…"

"But what?"

"She looks more like your granddaughter, sir. And they told us…"

"Told you what?"

"That Anna's brother had already passed away."

"Yes, everyone thinks I've been long gone, and that this marine town has already become a ghost town. If they did not think this, how can I protect the last few species living here?" The old man sighed and gestured us. "Will you both come in?"

"We can't, sir. We are fish."

"Oh, that's right. Alright, wait for me."

"Lynn, do you really think he is Anna's brother?"

"I don't know. Humans are devious creatures, Nerissa."

"Really? But humans are our god, Anna told me…"

"Shut up, Nerissa."

4

The old man with the silver hair told me that his name was Albert. Albert took us to a small pavilion and handed me a pack of dried fish fillets. Then, he began his story.

"In the year 2250, Anna, my grandmother, and I became the first citizens of Milana. Both our parents sacrificed themselves in a war between the Dutch and the robots. To repay us, the government selected us for immigration. Back then, I was only ten years old. My sister Anna was fifteen.

"Milana back then was just like how you would see it in propaganda. Every endangered marine species from each country was gathered. Every citizen signed an agreement: to prevent endangered species from torment. We all thought that this time we would learn our lesson and begin a better life, coexisting with our environment under the ocean, no longer fighting to survive. However, that did not last long. The year Anna turned twenty five, she could not stand the ocean's slow life. She secretly unlocked the border and slipped out — the mistake that spread chaos throughout."

"By 2260, Milana lost all peace. Carnivorous businessmen thirsting for the last drops of capital snuck in to satisfy their needs. The first massacre erupted, then another. The city became the supposed 'ghost town'. Nerissa, do you often hear low earthquake-like sounds battering the ridges down? That is the sound of war. The blood of our fellow marine species envelops our very city. We swore to protect them. But what would we do? All we could do was stand by helplessly as those creatures disappeared from our home, one by one."

"Where's the government? Why isn't the government doing anything?"

"The fight for natural resources on the land disintegrated all central government structures. Those who invaded and slaughtered our creatures were the same men who opposed spending billions of dollars to construct this sanctuary. When civil war broke out, the ones who supported us hid and dispersed across the world. How could they protect us when they could hardly survive themselves?"

"What about Anna, sir? Where did Anna go after she left the city?"

"My sister swam deeper and deeper into the ocean until the last slivers of light had slipped away from sight. That was when she discovered Edward's research facility. The moment she laid her eyes on Edward, she fell in love. But Edward was a famous scientist who only cared about saving the world. Why would he ever have eyes for the ordinary Anna?"

"Then what? What comes after?"

"Can you shut up Nerissa? Stop asking so many questions! Let Mr. Albert speak!"

"One month later, after Anna returned to the city and heard of the catastrophe, she ran away again. Everyone thought she ran because of her guilt, but I knew it was just her excuse to return to Edward. But what even I couldn't anticipate was how naive she was — so naive to give up her soul for him."

"What is 'soul'?"

"Shut up Nerissa, let Mr. Albert speak!"

"Soul, my sweet child, is your consciousness — an intangible difference between humans and robots. Yet Anna sacrificed her precious soul to Edward's robot experiment to stay with him forever. The Anna you saw, dear child, was Anna's soul within a fleshless robot casing."

"Wait! So you mean that the Anna who was always by my side was not a human? She was a robot?"

"Yes, my dear. She was a robot. A robot without flesh or bones."

"All of them were not human?"

"Yes, my dear. Edward never uses humans. He believes that their emotions will destroy his incredible work. He believes that he only needs logical robots to help him accomplish his goal to restore humanity. Truth is, he's right. Humans are full of sin. Our greed and lust will always kill all life, no matter how many second chances we're given."

"But sir, Anna never told me any of these stories about Milana. Anna only told me about her home. It is filled with sunlight and rose tea."

"Oh? Is that how she described it?" Albert laughed, his eyes slowly welling with tears. "That home is one we will never get to go back to again. It is now a wasteland. Do you know, my child, that 70% of the Earth's land is now a wasteland?"

"Why? What actually happened in the past fifty years?"

"War, my child. Ever occurring, constant warfare. Our planet was doomed the moment first world countries launched their nuclear missiles. We can never go back now. Even though Edward invented you, the fate of us humans is sealed."

"How can we fix this?" Lynn, who had been silent all this time spoke up.

"There's no way."

"Why?"

"Greed and lust have sealed our fate that no second chances can erase. They shut their bloody eyes to what we gained and crave after all that's left to raid. The earth, the sea, the sun, the rain. We make machines to defeat the vile monsters within ourselves, yet end up enslaving them as greater weapons to kill and sell. Child, I am well into sixty; there's not a lot of life left in me. With no off-spring to carry, I only have one wish... will you help me, please?"

"What is it, sir? We will do anything!"

"A hundred kilometers from Milana is Monaco, the most magnificent marine sanctuary. It may just be the only safe place in this world. I hope you can escort my dearest pet there. She is the last beluga whale left. I know that in a few years, she will pass away too, marking another extinction on this planet. But I hope that she can live out her last years freely and not locked up in this crystal cage like me."

"A whale! She must be huge! I've heard that whales are scary and will swallow us fish down in just one gulp!"

"No, my sweet child. Beluga whales are our friends. This one is already eight months old. Her mother was hunted last year, and a child needs their mother's milk to survive. I only have two more bottles of artificially produced milk. The only source left is in Monaco. My child, I beg you of this task. Please help me bring her back to safety."

"We will help you, dear sir. Do not worry!"

"Wait, Nerissa, you sure about that? If we leave now, there will be no turning back. And how do you think we can enter Monaco without all the hunters to see?"

"Lynn, aren't you the one who told me you don't want to be locked up in a cage forever? How can you let a fellow fish endure the same fate?"

"I never signed up for something we can't handle."

"So you are a scaredy-cat?"

"What? No."

"My child, I understand your dilemma. I will not force you if you don't want to."

"Not to worry, sir. I've made a promise. If Lynn does

not come along, I will go alone!"

"Oh Nerissa, you stubborn fish…"

Back then I had little doubt, because both humans and robots had always been kind and genuine. Perhaps if I hadn't made this promise, Lynn and I would still be swimming freely in Edward's lab.

I could never forget Albert's wrinkly emerald eyes — eyes like Anna's, glittering bright, and like that star lighting up the night we held Edward's corpse on the coast.

That brightest star, Edward told us, was Polaris.

5

Edward and his bots caught up to us not long after we bid farewell. I was not surprised. After all, if you didn't install tracking into your inventions, did you even do your job well?

This was the first time I met our inventor. He looked the same age as Albert, perhaps a bit older. How could a man of his age spend his remaining days in a lab, working away? Perhaps he really believed the world was his to save.

After we told Edward our plan, he was dismayed.

"Are you out of your mind? Your cells are not yet at all refined."

"Oh Edward, please! I'm begging you! This beluga whale deserves happiness too! You can't just rescue what you make! Help us just for Anna's sake!"

Edward paused when he heard Anna's name, a pensive look drawn on his face.

"Alright."

I could not believe what he just said. Edward had agreed to our plea! I thought he would bring us back. We wouldn't be able to resist if he had. I gurgled a billion bubbles in happiness.

Lynn did not share my sympathy and trembled his tail anxiously.

"Lynn, what's wrong?"

"I still don't think it's a good idea. Why don't we take the beluga to our home?"

"No, absolutely not. A pet beluga takes a lot. Our food is barely enough to feed you two. A full grown beluga whale will send our lab into ruins."

"Oh Edward, oh our dearest god, then please take us to Monaco, bring us with you and your bots! A hundred km is just a day and night's swim away. With you and your submarine, it'll be a piece of cake!"

"The distance is not the primary issue. It's the places we must pass through on our route. A city of blood and gunpowder comes between us and the shelter. I will help you, but promise this to me. After the trip, come back to my laboratory. Then never escape again into this dark and treacherous sea."

"Yes Edward, of course! We promise to be good!"

And off we went. Lynn, the beluga, and I swam in a line. Edward and his robots followed closely behind.

"Annie, my tortoise, farewell for now. I'm afraid I can't stick around."

"It's alright, Nerissa, let her go. I'll make a new one for you, improved just so."

"Make a new one?"

"Annie is a robot, it doesn't have a life like you. It is fake, Nerissa."

That was when I realized: all this time, all that I knew never really existed outside of my mind. But what really constitutes reality? Is it what fits into our rationality? Something that human logic can solve? If so, why is it that I love the fake so dearly?

Love, perhaps this is what Anna meant to love.

6

Fifty kilometers went by, and I started to falter behind. If I'd known one day I would swim a marathon, I would've followed Lynn's workout early on. Lynn saw my fatigue and stopped for a rest. But there wasn't a single safe place in this sea of darkness.

Edward stepped out of the submarine and swarm slowly towards me. His approaching figure seemed pretty fit for a man of almost seventy.

"My dearest mermaid children, come with me. There's a sky up there, do you want to see?"

Edward gently grasped our hands with his wrinkly fingers and began to swim up to the surface. That was the first time I touched human skin—the first time I touched human heat. I held onto him carefully, afraid to slip yet afraid to tear his fragility.

Figures slowly came into sight. The water glistened bright and tiny fish sparkled in the silvery light.

"We are almost there, my dear children. Remember you can stay for ten minutes only. Then you must return back to the sea. Do you understand?"

Tonight the moon looked like Edward's eyes, hanging crescent shaped in the sky. I gasped at the stunning sight.

"Edward, what are you looking at?"
"Looking at you. My dream had finally come true."
"What is your dream, Edward?"
"A long time ago, when I told Anna my mermaid goal, she would tell me the tale of *The Little Mermaid*. Now I look at you, and it's like the tale has come true."

"Edward, did you love Anna?"

Edward did not answer and instead raised his head to the sky. He pointed to a single small blinking light. A star — the only star in sight.

"Our ancestors believed that stars were our loved ones who had died. Every time you feel alone, just look up into the sky. Those who had passed will be watching and protecting you."
"Edward, do you believe that too?"
"No, I am a scientist. Fairytales are for the ordinary. I have dedicated my life to science, and the survival of our species. To me, sacrifice is the only means for some-

one to achieve great deeds."

"So you used science to keep her alive," Lynn replied.

"Yes, Lynn, that is right. It was my only way. When I pass away, I don't want a coffin. I will become immortal through technology and innovation."

"But Edward, your robots told me Anna will forever be asleep."

"She will come back."

"Edward, the singular star in the sky; does it have a name?"

"Humans call it Polaris. But it may disappear all the same. Within five years, we won't be able to see any stars with our naked eye."

"Edward, what is outside the sky?"

"It is called the universe."

"Can you tell me about what it does?"

"A hundred years ago, humans believed that it was the next destination we would go. Little did they know humanity was the cause of disparity. Wealth and fame, greed and selfishness, our sins have destroyed nearly everything. The fault, dear Nerissa, lies not within the stars, but in ourselves. But no more of this talk, time is up. We must return to the ocean. I will find a safe place for you two to rest."

"Lynn, do you think Polaris will disappear?" I nudged Lynn, who was already drifting asleep.

"If Edward said so, then I guess it's true," Lynn mumbled quietly.

"Do you think we will successfully complete Albert's task?"

"Yes, Nerissa, now relax. Stop thinking and go to sleep."

"I want you to hold me, I'm afraid."

"Alright I will hold you, now go to sleep. It is getting really late."

"Where is Edward and the beluga whale?"

"They should just be nearby."

"Lynn, I really don't want to fail."

"We won't. Trust that Edward will not lie."

"Lynn, I still can't sleep. Is there a song that you can sing?"

"I don't know how to sing."

"Yes you do, Lynn. Us mermaids can do anything."

"Alright, alright. I will sing you a song I heard from the crystal ball."

Lynn told me that this song was from three hundred years ago. As he sang, I heard in his voice a tinge of sorrow. I remembered the lyrics to be like this:

There's a place in your heart, and I know that it is love,
And this place could be much brighter than tomorrow.
There are ways to get there if you care enough for the living,
Make a little space, make a better place.

If you want to know why there's love that cannot lie,
Love is strong, and it only cares of joyful giving.
And the dream we were conceived in will reveal a joyful face,
And the world we once believed in will shine again in grace.

Heal the world, make it a better place,
For you and for me and the entire human race.
There are people dying if you care enough for the living,
Make it a better place for you and for me.

For you and for me.

7

The next day was the first time I was awakened by light. Lynn promised me a feast for breakfast last night. However, he was nowhere in my sight. The thought of breakfast made my stomach growl. I leapt out of the water in excitement. Behind wisps of clouds was a fiery sphere of light.

That must be the sun!

Across the sea, I saw the horizon line. The water there seemed to be of a different kind. It was deep red and scattered with dark clusters, gurgling and rumbling from behind.

Then I remembered Albert's words: that was the sound of war.

Lynn was not here. Edward and the beluga was also nowhere near. I started to worry anxiously.

I dove back into the ocean and found Edward's submarine in about a thousand meters. But what caught my
attention was another ship. An uneasy feeling clenched
my gut as I hid behind a giant sea kelp. I peeked through
the slivers cautiously, preparing myself to rush to help.

The hatch to the foreign ship slammed open and I saw a
familiar figure. It was Albert! Oh, what a relief! He must
be just checking up on his beluga buddy!

As I swished my tail, ready to come out from my hiding
place, I saw Albert approach with a row of robots, a
solemn look on his face.

"Hello Edward, I am Albert. After so many years, we
finally meet."
"Hello Albert, may I help you?"
"I came to check up on my beluga whale. How's she
doing?"
"She's doing great. And since you're here, you can
take over and escort her to Monaco yourself. We'll step
out from here."
"Don't leave just yet, Edward. I came to discuss a
deal."

I felt a tap on my back.

"Oh my gosh Lynn, you scared me!" I whispered
quietly. "Where did you go?"
"To find breakfast for you. Didn't I say so?"
"Then where is my breakfast?"

"Couldn't find any food. Not a single shrimp in the last a hundred meters, two hundred too. But guess what I saw in the neighboring sea?"

"What did you see?"

"Not telling you."

"You selfish!"

"So what's happening there?"

"I don't know, I feel a bit scared. What do you think he wants, Lynn?"

"Give me Lynn and Nerissa, and I'll leave your legacy in tact."

"I beg your pardon?"

"Think of it as a generous offer, as you never gave my sister back. You tricked then exploited her poor soul just to make the first conscious robot model."

"Anna volunteered on her own."

"No! You gave her hope! You made her believe she could be with you forever!" Albert grew increasingly emotional.

I saw the robots behind him lift their rifles. I felt I should do something, something brave and something bold.

"Where are you going, Nerissa? Are you out of your mind?"

"I have to stop him! Edward loved Anna! Come help me, we can sneak up from behind!"

"Don't be stupid! Just because a human says something doesn't mean it's what they really meant."

"Albert, take your beluga whale and go. We are both not children anymore. Let's not act like such. We can forget all this ever happened."

"I can't leave. We both can't leave."

"What did you do?"

"It's either my beluga whale or your mermaids, I'm sorry. I don't have any other family. She is everything to me. Yesterday after your mermaids left, they found me while I was holding the tracker in my hand. This is our decided fate that both of us can no longer escape."

I felt the ocean tremor so slightly only us fish can sense. Lynn felt it too and shot me a glance.

"Let's go now, Nerissa, let's go with caution. I think more tanks are coming this direction."

"No! What about Edward? We are fast swimmers. We can swim over and rescue him!"

"No listen to me, don't be silly. Just go, as fast as you can, right behind me."

Lynn was too strong, and I knew I shouldn't cause too much commotion. I was dragged away unwillingly.

"They are coming from the city. We must enter the sea region now."

"Which sea?"

"I call it the death sea: a sea of bones and bodies decomposing."

8

"Lynn, do you think they will catch up to us?"

I swam, turning back nervously. I dreaded that, at any moment, I would see those vast ships and they would swallow up us two little fish.

"We are cold-blooded animals. Regular biodetectors cannot trace us. Don't look back. You have to trust me, Nerissa."

"But Edward...we're all that he has..."

"The one thing Edward would wish right now is for his inventions to last."

The smell of blood flooded around us the closer we approached the death sea. The ocean bled red like a freshly cut gash. Different pieces of trash darkened the sea like ash, smashing into us. I tried to avoid the whiplash of plastic against my head, but still caught myself strangled in a tangle of junk. I gasped for air, yelling for Lynn's name. Lynn heard my cry and quickly came, pulling the plastic bag off my head.

"Are you stupid! This region is a warzone!" he looked furious. "You've gotta be more serious and focus on where you're going. Follow me closely, and don't stop swimming!"

Not a sign of living creatures was in sight as we ventured onwards into the death sea. It was as if Lynn had already been to the area before. He quickly found a sea rock close to the shore.

"You guessed this would happen, didn't you?"

Lynn didn't say a word. He hovered over me and shielded me against the rubble ammunition. At that moment, I felt his affection. Although we were cold-blooded animals, I felt his heat against me.

"Lynn, I'm scared."
"Scared of what?"
"Scared that we're going to die."
"Not to worry. I'm here."

Lynn and I silently curled together as the sky slowly lost its light.

"Now what, Lynn, what should we do?"
"Let's go find Edward and maybe Albert too."

Before we left the death sea, I decided to give the surface a peak. Lynn hesitated to let me, glancing up indecisively.

"Are you sure this is what you want to do?"
"Yes, positive. I have to."

The next few moments changed my life and defined all of what I stood for. Thousands of human and fish corpses floated onto the surface, laced with mold, sparkling against the scarlet sea foam.

That was the moment when I knew all that glisters is not gold.

Heartbroken, I scooped up a sagging angelfish with drooping scales. He stared back at me with charcoal eyes and weakly jiggled its tail with the last of his life.

"Don't be afraid, buddy. Go to sleep. Your next life will be all flowers and rose tea," I took him into my embrace. The angelfish struggled just a little, then seemed to understand my words. It stopped fighting and went away, like thousands of his confederates.

"Nerissa, time to let him go. He belongs to the ocean. It is his home."

I let him go unwillingly. The fish's golden belly flipped up, then slowly drifted away with the others to the shore. There awaited hundreds of vultures for their meals to arrive. I guess these were the only lives who could survive this atrocity.

"We must keep moving," Lynn dragged me back to the ocean. "I bet Albert was tricked by them as well. Monaco is probably falling to enemy occupation just about now."

"Oh no! What will happen to the poor fish there?"

"Worry more about yourself for now."

"But we have to help them, Lynn!"

"Don't be a fool. Save yourself before saving the world."

9

Perhaps all is crueler in reality. I knew that two mer-maids had nothing against this everlasting war between the mechanic and the living. On our trip back, I wished desperately for Edward and Albert to be alive. Their lives meant hope for all of us.

They must survive, they must.

I could nurture Albert and his beluga whale back in our lab. "I am willing to eat less shrimp or just seaweed," I thought to myself. "The beluga whale is still growing. She will need nutrition more than me." I remembered her smiling eyes and glossy forehead nudging ours, as if we were of the same bloodline.

I wanted to tell Edward that he was right and I would never leave his side again. Lynn and I were grownups now, and we would take care of him from now on.

Edward was taking his last breath as we approached his limestone death bed. He looked as if his body would give away, threatening to disintegrate. The robots nursing his wounds shook their heads and slowly powered down. Albert and the beluga whale were also nowhere to be found.

"Edward, let us take you to your lab. You will get better there."

"Not to worry my child, do not fear for what I have waiting for me. Take me to the surface of the sea. I want to see the moon one last time."

In the night sky, the moon and Polaris fought to glow behind the thicket of dark smoke. Under the soft diffused moonlight, Lynn held Edward in his arms while I clutched onto his wrinkly palms. Edward's eyes were rimmed with tears, like the angelfish, waiting for the death approaching near.

"It's over my child. The era of humanity is gone."

"Don't say that Edward, you will live on. Promise me you will survive and go on to save all our lives."

"Nerissa, remember my words. Love mankind: they are your god. Love your own: they are your peers. Love the ocean: it is your home. And most importantly, you must love every living creature in the sea. This is now your responsibility. Promise me."

"Edward, please don't go. You are our god. You can't leave us."

"Don't cry, my dear Nerissa, do not fuss. If you miss

me, look up and find that brightest star. I will always be watching you from afar. I will make a promise to you now. Before the last star disappears from the sky, I will return to your side."

"But Edward, I thought you didn't believe in fairy-tales…"

Edward never said a word again. His eyelids drooped slowly upon his emerald eyes. A single tear escaped and rolled down his cheek. I held him gently until the warmth slipped out of his body. Lynn held me tightly, whispering. The pain I felt was newfound back then. I was confused and filled with resent. How much hate must one have to put another's life to end? How many souls must they conquer until they are fully content?

I did not understand love or death before leaving my glass cage. With age, I began to comprehend. But that only made me understand that ignorance is bliss.

10

On the first day of the 24th century, two hundred days after Edward had gone, I finally recorded my story down. We kept Edward in his pre-planned body, and left to set upon a wandering journey.

Edward had another secret gift for us. Our lab turned out to be a giant submarine that camouflages, hiding us deep in the sea, away from all our enemies.

"How many human secrets are there to know?"

"Just enough so. But as for this secret, only to us had Edward told. Edward long knew of today's arrival. We must follow his command and leave this location for us to continue our survival."

"Will Edward ever wake up again?"

"We don't know, but he did make a promise. You should trust in what Edward had said."

We then set out for our wandering journey. Lynn and I

began on a mission. We gathered robot sea turtles and robot fish, and rescued all dying sea creatures. I spotted a dolphin twisted and torn by metal rings. I gave him a name— "Usha" — the Hindu for dawn and new beginnings.

Oh, I almost forgot to mention: I gave birth to two boys and three girls, carrying on Edward's invention. When I was pregnant, Lynn gave me much more attention, becoming much more caring and patient. But I felt that he lost a part of himself nonetheless and became constantly serious and cautious. He liked to visit the front cockpit, sitting to discuss with the robot team about our upcoming passage. Sometimes, he crouched alone in front of the control panel and stared blankly at coordinates and radio channels.

I would often grow frustrated at his monotonous melancholy. He would only reply blatantly, "I cannot risk to put in danger you, our children and all of nature."

But the old Lynn returned a few times during each day. When I was pregnant, he stuck his bald head against my belly and listened to what our unborn children would say.

"Lynn, stop listening. You're crushing them."
"Shh, listen. They are saying daddy!"
"Don't be stupid. They can't talk if they're not born yet."

Fortunately for me, my mermaids were born smoothly.

Lynn wove five bracelets of coral and algae and slipped them on their tiny wrists as they were sleeping. I'd always wondered how gleeful Edward and Anna would be if they could see that my five mermaids would survive and create generations after generations to thrive.

Will Lynn and I be ancestors to a mermaid family? Will we become a legacy, written down for the future to read?

How will they tell our stories after a few hundred centuries?

Lynn emerged from behind and brought me to Edward's glass confine. "Hey Nerissa, look who's back?" I gasped and laughed with grateful tears. Lynn put a hand over my cheers. "Let them rest a little more."

Will Edward be impressed when he sees all that I've created and saved?

But is it enough to pave the way, to heal from all of Earth's dismay?

"Lynn."
"Yes, Nerissa?"
"Our descendants are here and they are awake. I want to do something I've always feared."
"What is it?"
"Lynn, do you want to be locked up in a cage forever?"
"Nerissa…"

"Lynn, are you a scaredy-cat?"
"Nerissa, you are the biggest idiot."

Lynn grabbed my hand and off we swam, passing by all that now thrived and flourished. I glanced back to see those marine creatures that we nourished turning back to watch us go, I swished my eighteen rows of scales — bidding adieu.

"Lynn, where are we going?"
"Shut up, Nerissa."

I am Nerissa, a first-generation mermaid. At the turn of the 24th century, I return back into the vast sea. I no longer feared for the violence and blood that killed our Earth's diversity. But please forgive me for one deed.

Today, I will no longer write my story. If the future continues in war, please keep what you just read a secret for me. But if the future comes to a rest, please find our secret ship's address. Please give Edward our apologies for leaving so improperly. Please tell him we thank him for creating us, and that we love him as long as time lasts.

"Lynn, sing me a song?"
"I don't know how to sing."
"Yes you do. The one you've sung to me."
"Okay, Nerissa."

There's a place in your heart, and I know that it is love,
And this place could be much brighter than tomorrow.

There are ways to get there if you care enough for the living,
Make a little space, make a better place.

If you want to know why there's love that cannot lie,
Love is strong and it only cares of joyful giving.
And the dream we were conceived in will reveal a joyful face,
And the world we once believed in will shine again in grace.

Lynn squeezes my fingers as we venture into the lingering darkness of the sea. I don't know where we'll go next, but I know that we'll have an effect on the dying Earth ahead. We have a responsibility to carry: to love and save every living creature in the sea. I don't know where we will go next, I just know I'm no longer a test subject. I am Nerissa, the mother of the new sea. And I exist truly and willfully.

Heal the world, make it a better place,
For you and for me and the entire human race.
There are people dying if you care enough for the living,
Make it a better place for you and for me.

For you and for me.

For you and for me.

- *FIN* -

Bobo

"I don't have a planet. My existence is a continuum that consists of thousands of possibilities. Some are big, some are small; some I'm here, some I'm there."

- Bobo, Chapter 7

1

I was hiding out on a toilet seat in the boy's bathroom. On my lap perched my bento box holding my mama's garlic chives and white cabbage pork dumplings. The chives were pungent. The blonde girl sitting next to me in math class told everyone I had rotten food in my backpack. I tried to explain, but she wouldn't listen.

"Look everyone, Bobo brought garbage for lunch again!" she cackled as she tossed her mustard blonde hair.
"It's a kind of Chinese vegetable," I stuttered with my Chinese accent, racking my brain for the words to describe chives.
"You stunk up my new outfit! This garbage belongs in the trash!"
"Sorry, sorry."

My cheeks flushed. I grabbed my Adidas bag and retreated to a quiet corner in the back. I watched as the hands on the clock crawled ever so slowly along their tracks, praying for the bell to release me from this cage.

I shoved a dumpling into my mouth. The skin had gone cold and stiff and had congealed into a huge tasteless lump. That blonde girl was right: this was garbage. Left-overs were garbage and should be thrown into the trash.

My name is not "Bobo". I'm Steven. Steven Sheng. There are millions of Stevens in this world. When your parents don't know what name to give their son, Steven becomes a default, along with all the other Alexs, Johns, and Adams. No offense. And I definitely had lived up to the mediocrity of my name. I was as mediocre as my name. "He looks like an earnest and hardworking guy," they would say. "His grades must be stellar!"

Why must they judge a book by its cover? Sorry to disappoint, but neither did I have good grades nor did I pursue any hobbies. The only thing I was good at was asking myself silly existential questions that no one could answer.

Who am I? Why am I myself and not someone else? Why do I exist in this world?

I transferred from my school in Hangzhou, China to Rudemon High, located in a small town in Texas. It was a month into my move when I realized that life in this country was nothing like the movies. Skyscrapers and neon signs were really colorful tents of the homeless dotting the bare, lifeless streets. The Chinese food here wasn't even Chinese food. Panda Express. Their food was as lame as their name. All they had were broccoli beef and sweet and sour chicken. What an insult to our rich and storied tradition. I hoped that, one day, Americans could have a taste of braised pork belly and West Lake fish in vinegar gravy. Then they would have a semblance of what real Chinese food — what real *food* — tastes like.

Including myself, there were only three Chinese students in Rudemon High. Cindy and Vanie, the other two Chinese girls, were as exotic as my caucasian classmates. I thought I could have a fresh start here, but instead I found myself with no friends, yet again. Not to worry. I grew up invisible anyways. Really, I embraced the loneliness. It gave me time to rethink my existence. While other immigrants wanted to live out their version of the American dream, all I wanted to do was to be left alone.

Unfortunately, even that became a luxury.

The seniors in the school always gave the new kid a nickname. "Bobo" was what they called me.

> *Bobo, bobo, what do you know?*
> *Why did China let you go?*
> *Why are you here in America?*
> *Don't communists have bananas?*

I couldn't understand them back then, but I was no fool.

I saw the scorn in their eyes, taunting me with every step I took. They loathed me, but not just me as a person. They loathed my identity. They loathed my country, my traditions, my food. Even so, I was too afraid to defend myself.

"Thank you, thank you," I would reply.

"Thank you" was among the few words I actually knew how to say. They would always record my stutters, snickering hysterically behind their Nokia flip phones. Back in the early 2000s, those flashy metal bricks were signs for class and status. Their gossip spread like wildfire, destroying my humble way of life. Every time it seemed the fire was waning, another press of their clunky plastic triggers would drop a new wave of kindling, reinvigorating their taunts. Hunting nobodies like me was their sport of choice.

I heard the bell of hell crackle through the half-broken speakers above me. I chucked the remainder of my lunch into the toilet and pulled out a piece of crumpled class schedule from my Adidas bag, my prized possession gifted to me on my 11th birthday.

I hated Mondays. It was the day where all my boring classes were grouped together. I hated my science teacher, Mr. Nevinson. Bald Voldemort was what I called him. Picking on me was his favorite pastime, so I always tried my best not to be late.

I rushed out of the bathroom and found a nice corner of the classroom to claim. Sunlight cascaded in through the glass window that separated me from freedom.

That's when I saw it: a weird squiggle on the desk in the corner of my eye.

2

The squiggle looked like a planet entangled in kaleidoscopic rings. Above the drawing was a short English phrase. Despite my atrocious English, the line was simple enough to understand.

"Who am I?" it read.

I became entranced. Wasn't this the question that I've always sought the answer to? *Who am I?* I lapsed into a deep reverie, pondering the question.

"Steven!"
"Here, here!" I shot up in my seat, the plastic neon chair clattering behind me.

"You can't even recognize your own name?"

The classroom burst into hysterical laughter.

"Sorry. Sorry."

"Alright students, ready for the first day of October? This month we will be discussing the origins of mankind. First row, please pass down the worksheet. I believe that most of you are aware that our ancestors were apes. Now, let us travel back two million years…"

Mr. Nevinson's lesson was hypnotic. His voice was like a metronome mechanically reciting the textbook line by line. It might sound like a joke to you, but here's something I've always thought. Science must be borne of human delusion. All of these formulas we now take for objective truth, once only existed in someone's imagination. The better you can turn your delusions into formulas, the better chance you have of winning a Nobel Prize.

How in the world could we possibly prove what happened two million years ago? How arrogant must we be to believe we can control the past and the future?

To prevent myself from falling asleep during the unremitting chanting, I began examining the sketch. Was this a prank? Or was there a hidden message for me to decipher? I was horrifically bored, so I pulled out a pencil and added a line.

"Who are you?" I scribbled with my crooked handwriting. I actually wanted to ask, "What does the drawing mean?" but I couldn't find the appropriate English words in my mental dictionary.

"Steven!"
"Here, here!"
"Do me a favor and hand in your notes, will you?"
"Sorry teacher…"
"You didn't finish it again?"

Mr. Nevinson sighed. The recess bell rang, and I scurried out of that hell hole, my Adidas bag trailing behind me.

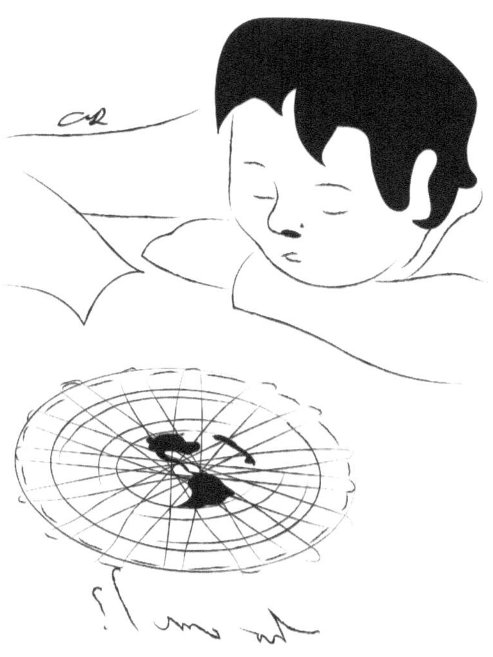

3

ESL class might have been the only place where I actually felt visible. Besides me, Vanie, and Cindy, there were two Indians who were even lower on the food chain than me. They weren't only bullied by the seniors but also the Mexican juniors. "Indians smell because they never take showers" was the rumor.

Vanie and Cindy left arm in arm to go to the bathroom, again. They loved sticking together. As the famous Chinese writer Lu Xun once wrote, "Livestock travel in herds, the vicious remain solo." Although I was not a beast, I would often wonder whether my solitude would create the cocoon for my metamorphosis.

Maybe, just maybe, I could one day become the hunter and not the prey.

"Steven, what's your favorite clothing brand?"
"I don't know… Adidas?"

I had tried my best to join in on the girls' gushings about Juicy Couture and Abercrombie & Fitch. Naturally, I failed. Even if I did befriend them, "Playboy Bobo" would become my new moniker.

I felt bad for them as they spent every day obsessing over the inconsequential. Fact is, they were in the same boat as me: people who had no agency over their own existence.

"Steven, look at your idiot face and ugly clothes," they always chortled. "You will never find a girlfriend, ever."

Oh I'm sorry I'm not dating K-pop stars like you guys are… oh wait, you guys aren't either.

When no one was watching, I flipped open my notebook and carefully sketched the drawing from the classroom table. The planet initially looked like Jupiter, but I became more and more convinced that the planet was actually Earth.

But what were the shapes that orbited it?

"Steven, are you drawing? What is it?"
"Stop it Cindy. Give it back!"
"What the heck is this? Vanie, look at this! This looks like a drawing by a two-year-old! Are you two, Bobo?"
"Steven, are you becoming like mentally retarded? Don't spend so much time alone. It will make you para-

noid."

"Give it back!" I mustered up my most intimidating voice to reprimand them.

"Steven is mad! He looks exactly like a bobo when he's angry!"

Ugh, I really hated Rudemon High.

4

When I returned to science class the next day, I was pleasantly surprised to find a reply under my question. Although I couldn't quite understand it, I carefully copied it down in my agenda. When the recess bell rang, I ran to the library and turned on a Dell. I clumsily typed in those strange glyphs into a Chino-English dictionary.

"Borrow a book with the serial number E-S201."

I rushed to the librarian's desk.

"Sorry, I need ... this, this number."
"Looking for a book with this serial number?"
"Yes, yes!" I exclaimed.

The librarian led me to the dustiest shelf tucked away in the back corner. He took out a thick hardcover book and handed it to me. It was a dry nonfiction read, with a golden cover that resembled the sketch on my table.

"Thank you, thank you!"

"This book is for advanced readers. Perhaps this would be more suitable." the black man with a large bushy beard enunciated each syllable as if I was hard of hearing. He flicked a crooked finger towards the children's book section, with a fake smile plastered on his face.

"Thank you, bye." I mumbled, eyes trained on the glimmering cover.

"Alright then," he sighed contemptuously as he shuffled slowly back to his seat.

I clutched the book in my chest and ran towards the bus station. Some seniors blocked me halfway and encroached upon me.

"What's up communist Bobo? Let's hear a roar."

"What?"

"I want you to roar like this," they made some screeching sounds. "Understand?"

"*Roarrrr.*" I did exactly as they said.

They howled, the meat shaking on their starch white bodies, then slithered away on their skateboards. Fortunately, they were too busy tormenting me to notice the book in my arms.

"Hey son, are you back?"

"Yes, mama."

"How was school?"

Pointless question.

"Pretty good." I repeated for the millionth time.

"Dinner is ready. Finish these chive dumplings and study in your room. Remember to sleep at ten!"

"Mama, can we not have chive dumplings in the future?" I cautiously tested the waters. "My classmates say they smell weird."

"Where did you learn to become such a picky eater? It took hours to make these dumplings. Good sons obey their mothers. I quit my job and sacrificed everything for you. How many mothers are there in the world that would sacrifice everything for their children? You…"

"Okay mama, forget it. I'm sorry."

"Eat them all and go study. Don't sleep until you finish 100 pages of your grammar practice."

I wanted to defend myself, but the first thing that prey learn is to run, not fight. It is a way of self-preservation. Moments like these reminded me of my pathetic existence. Everyone had to contribute to society in some way. My role was to be a circus monkey for the seniors, and a well-behaved pet for my mama.

At least that was what I thought back then.

My bedroom was my safe space. I laid on my bed and stared at the ceiling until a voice broke the silence.

"Open the book," it whispered from far away.

I startled and leapt out of bed. Vanie was right, I must be paranoid.

"You aren't crazy. Open the book. Yes, the book you borrowed from the library."

I hesitated for a second before I shakily opened the book.

"Oh I'm finally here!"

Now the voice was whispering directly into my ear.

"Who in the world are you?"
"Who in the world are you?"
"I'm asking you!"
"I'm asking you!"

Ugh, he sounded like a parrot.

"I'm not a parrot, but I know you are bobo."
"How do you know my nickname?"

I began to think that I had gone crazy. I tried to cover my ears and block out his voice. Little did I know that the voice came from deep within me. Covering my ears only amplified its audaciousness.

"Who are you?" I asked once more.
"I am you," it replied.
"Who am I?"

The voice grew silent.

"Who are you and who am I! Answer me!"
"You are Steven, and you are not Steven. I am you and you are me. You can't touch me but you can hear me."
"What the heck are you talking about."
"You are me, but only a part of me."

The voice echoed in my head.

"You are me, but only a part of me," I repeated in my head.

5

This was the most ridiculous thing I had ever encountered in my life. Since that day, I became possessed by that other "me".

"So you're Steven?"

"I am Steven, but I am also not Steven."

"What's your name?"

"In every universe, I have a different name. On earth, my name is Steven."

"I can't just call you 'the other Steven'. You need to have a name."

"I don't mind you giving me a name."

I thought for a second, "Tiga."

"Why?"

Ultraman Tiga was my favorite TV show in the early 2000s. I've always dreamed of becoming a superhero like him: versatile and inhumanly strong, shielding the world from chaos and invasion.

"Ok, Tiga, let me get this clear. You are me, and I am a part of you. Steven is only one of the thousands of names that you have in this universe."
"Correct. You are smart, Steven."

Wow, that was the first time I heard a sincere compliment coming from… myself.

I poured myself some oatmeal.

"Human food on Earth is weird. It all looks like swine feed."
"Disgusting, huh? It's called oatmeal and I hate it, but my mama told me it's healthy. Apparently it's what Americans have for breakfast everyday: oatmeal plus a peanut butter sandwich. So what do you eat, Tiga?"
"I don't have to eat."
"Huh?"
"Only creatures from three-dimensional spaces have to eat."

Tiga piqued my curiosity. I carefully pulled out the book on the bus. I typed nearly every word into my electronic dictionary, straining to understand what it meant.

"Trying to understand the book?"
"Didn't you come from the book? Can't you tell me about it?"

"Look at the cover, what do you see?"

"A planet that looks... trapped."

"You are smart, Steven."

"Trapped in what?"

"It's not the Earth that's trapped. It's you, Steven."

He was right. I was the planet, locked in the cage for barbarians while the beasts roamed freely about.

"But it's okay, Steven. Think of your life as a sort of simulation game, where the only thing you can prove to exist is yourself."

"What's a simulation game? Like The Sims 2? I really want it for my birthday, but my mama says excessive gaming destroys discipline."

"Well, you can think of your life as a more advanced version of the Sims. I know you can't accept it but it's the truth."

"Can you prove it?"

"I can't, but it's the truth."

"It is not the truth if you can't prove it."

"I can prove it, but I can't prove it to you. Otherwise I'll be violating the Parallel Universal Law No. 2132. But remember my words. The only thing you can prove to exist is yourself."

"The only thing I can prove to exist is myself," I thought about it over and over in my head, trying to understand its significance.

In science class, Mr. Nevinson began rambling on about

human evolution. "Our human ancestors speciated from the ancestors of the gorillas. The first anatomically modern humans are called Homo sapiens. They appeared in Africa some time before 100kY."

"That is incorrect," Tiga whispered in my ear. "People on earth like making funny assumptions."

"So who is my ancestor? Where did I come from?"

"Believe it or not, Steven, I put you here."

"You're talking nonsense."

"It's true, I put you here. It's an experiment."

"Excuse me? So I'm just a subject in your experiment?"

"No Steven. You are me, remember?"

"This is getting absurd. Are you an alien? Where's your planet?"

"I don't have a planet."

"What do you mean you don't have a planet?"

"I live in a higher dimension, so I don't need a planet."

"What does it look like?"

"It doesn't have a 'look', just one big fog of consciousness."

"Everything has a look. Even bacteria has a look."

"No, that's not true. Only creatures on earth care about their looks."

"If you don't have a look, then you're just a ghost or a spirit. In fact, even ghosts and spirits have looks. I see them in horror movies all the time."

"Ghosts and spirits do have an appearance because they are in a lower dimension than me."

What Tiga said reminded me of my Buddhist mama. When I was young, she told me that there are three levels of our world. There is the world of desire, where ghosts, humans, and animals coexist. There is the world of form, where dhyāna-dwelling gods live free of desires. There is the world of formlessness, the highest dimension, where immortal celestials reside. I always thought my mama was out of her mind and that these were only myths passed down by ignorant idiots who probably believed the world is flat.

"Oh what, so now you are telling me you're like a god?"

"Why do you sound angry? I am just answering your questions."

"Shut up and leave me alone, freak. Get out of my head!" I yelled. Suddenly, a million eyeballs turned to stare at me. And I became the circus monkey awkwardly standing under the center of the spotlight, again.

"Steven, sounds like you have something to say to my lesson?"

"No, teacher. Sorry."

"Mr. Nevinson, Bobo just interrupted the class! He has to apologize."

"I think that's correct," bald Voldemort's head bobbed up and down. "Steven, interrupting without raising your hand is rude. Do you understand?"

"Sorry, sorry" was all I replied.

I sat down, ears flushed red. That was the moment I realized I had the magical ability to turn off Tiga's voice in my head. "Who does he think he is?" I thought to myself. "Did he fly all this way to humiliate me? How did he get here anyways? Don't aliens live millions of light years away from earth?"

I was furious. I could feel the voice trying squirm back, seeking to explain himself. I refused to give him a second chance. He understood nothing about the human race. All he was trying to prove was his superiority.

"I am nothing," I thought to myself. "Just a pathetic experimental subject of him. I was meant to endure all this unfairness because that's what pleased him."

I thought I won, but I was wrong. That night, Tiga returned in a way that I would never forget.

6

It was a weird dream. I floated in the air as I heard a spiritual voice calling my name softly. "Come, Steven," he called. "Let me show you the truth."

The more I tried to focus, the more I lost grip on my sanity. I fell into a kaleidoscope as my consciousness splintered into fragments, clustering into a singular dot bathed in a phosphorescence.

It was a city of climbing skyscrapers, folding atop each other in organic lines. On the streets, gleaming silver giants cast elongated shadows onto the metal ground. Even higher up in the sky, dinosaurs soared over cumulus clouds whiter than the purest snow I'd ever seen. Suddenly, the collosal, glistening world collapsed, crashing to the ground. A monstrous wave rose above the debris, swallowing the once extraordinary earth.

Gasping for air, sputtering and choking from the seawater, I furiously struggled to keep afloat. The ocean waves lapped against my chin. A swarm of aluminum spheres knocked me back underwater with a splash. I desperately kicked my legs, forcing myself back to the surface. As I once again emerged, a blazing sunlight blinded my sight. No, that was not the sun.

The swarm of aluminum spheres had converged into cluster of piercing reflections on the ocean's horizon. I squinted to decipher what they were, but was suddenly ripped away from the water.

I tumbled out of the Earth, sailing further and further away until the Earth, then the Milky Way, then all of the universe concentrated into a singular glowing sphere of light. The light plunged into infinity until all that was left was darkness. Zero. Nothing. I stumbled backwards in shock, only to realize that I no longer could stumble. I grasped for myself, yet could not move or feel. I frantically looked around, only to see pure obscurity. I screamed, yet could not make a sound.

All that was left was a thunderous roar of silence.

"Wake up Steven. Didn't you hear your alarm clock? You are gonna be late for school!" my mama dragged me out of my blanket. "Why are you holding a book? Since when did you become so hardworking?"

I opened my eyes to find myself back in reality. But what really was reality? I knew there was only one person who could answer my question. That is, if he could be considered as a person.

But he was gone. I couldn't feel his existence anywhere. Was I too harsh yesterday? Or was the dream his final goodbye? Now I was convinced that he was here to reveal some dark secret about the human race, and that it was my destiny to spread the revelation to the public.

Foolishly, that's what I did. I couldn't imagine how I had the courage to stand up and confront bold Voldemolt.

"I am against the evolution theory" I shouted with my shaky English.

"That's because you have never evolved, Bobo!" they mocked. Hysterical laughter followed.

I froze there with my legs shaking restlessly under the desk. My fingers clenched into two fists. The pain of my nails digging into my palm kept me from fainting. I could feel my back wet with sweat.

"Stay calm, they are all just vultures who feast on other's suffering. Do not pass out. They are idiots," I chanted to myself. "Do not pass out. Do not pass out. Stupid. Idiots."

A few hours later, I proved myself to be right. I could never forget the excruciating cold when the seniors dumped a bucket of ice water onto my head, crushing my self-esteem.

"Bobo, we heard you love eating on the toilet. Here's our gift, do you love it?"

"No, no!" I shouted, my body shivering helplessly.

"Don't pollute our school with your stinky breath, be obedient or go back to your country and starve to death!"

"No, no!" There was an abundance of food in my homeland. What kind of a stereotypical assumption was that?

It took me a century to dry my hair and clothes under the hand dryer.

"Steven!" Cindy called outside the boy's bathroom. "The seniors are drawing all over your locker. I was too afraid to stop them. You should go take a look."

"What should I do?" I desperately closed my eyes. "Go tell them to stop the nonsense? Run straight to the principal's office?"

I regretted my decision the moment I stepped out of the bathroom. They were waiting for me, with their metal Nokias locked and loaded.

"I'm sorry Steven, they told me so," Cindy slipped away with her guilty eyes.

I must have looked like a drowned mouse, stuck in the mouse trap and staring up at the perpetrator's blinding flashlight. "Why are you doing this?" I wanted to ask. "Does intimidating me make you feel better? Proving your self-worthiness by fooling a new student? How pathetic!"

"Please, don't. Sorry, sorry…" was all I had the courage to say. My voice faded in their song:

Bobo, bobo, what do you know?
Why did China let you go?
Why are you here in America?
Don't communists have bananas?

I was too weak and naive back then. I couldn't understand what made them hate me so much, but as I grew up I began to realize, democracy was the only system they were taught to be authentic and prominent. Communism to them was a derogatory term, savage and dreadful. When I heard them use these words to attack me over and over again, I lost the strength to even say no. I began to despise my nation and my race. "If I am not Chinese," I told myself, "I wouldn't be treated with such cruelty."

When I finally returned home, I locked myself in my room. I took out the golden book from my Adidas bag, and carefully opened it.

"Come back, Tiga," I murmured. "I need you."

No reply.

"Come back, please?" I tried again.

Tick tock. The ticking antique clock mirrored my quivering heartbeat.

"Do you know, Tiga? You are my only friend."

7

I was sitting in Principal Smith's office with my mama next to me.

"Are you aware that your son is misbehaving in school?" Mr. Smith asked sternly. "Due to his offensive speech toward Mr. Nevinson, we have decided to give out a warning."

"What did he say, son? Did you do something wrong at school?" my mama whispered.

"Can I explain it to you after we get home?" I carefully picked my words.

"Can you understand me, M'am? Our students told me that your son rudely offended his science teacher during lecture. We understand that he is still adapting to the environment, but we do hope he can cause no more chaos in the school. If the situation gets worse in the future, we might have to suspend or repatriate him."

"Yes, sorry," My mama nodded, although I knew she didn't understand a word he said.

"Steven, do you understand what you did wrong? I know you are new to Rudemon High and new to American culture, but you have to learn to behave and respect others."

"Sorry, teacher. I will, I will."

I was ashamed. I hated myself for the inability to speak up. My mama grabbed me from the principal's office and took me straight back home. After I told my her the truth, she did not sympathize with me. She insisted that it was me who misbehaved. To shut me up, she hit me hard with her broom. I kneeled down onto the ground, speechless.

"I am a strong young man." I told myself. "I shall not weep or shed a single tear."

"I am so disappointed in you! I gave up everything for you, and this is how you thank me? Do you know how many people dream of studying in America? Do you know how much we spent, how many people we begged to get you the student visa?"

"I told you mama, I did nothing wrong. Why don't you trust me? I am your son!"

"Why are you still quibbling? Are you saying that the school was lying?"

"He is racist! They all are!"

"Shut up now! How can I raise a son like you?"

My mama started to sob, but I was not in the mood to comfort her. I grabbed my Adidas bag, swung it behind my back, then slammed the door behind me. I started running down the lifeless gravel road, faster and faster. An hour later, I found myself at the edge of a cliff, overlooking the sea. The sun behind the silky smooth clouds turned into scarlet red, and the waves roared in despair.

"How beautiful this scene is, how beautiful it is just a jump below," I thought to myself. "If Tiga was telling the truth, if my life was an experiment all along, I think I should end all the suffering and move on."

"So you are giving up?" A familiar voice whispered beside my ears. "I don't think it's time to give up, Steven."

"You are back, Tiga! Oh thank god you are back! Where have you been? Why did you leave without saying goodbye? Why were you not here when I needed you? You are my only friend!"

"It's funny how you consider me to be your friend, Steven. You and I are one, remember? But, I don't mind being your friend, if that makes you feel better. Now, Steven, listen carefully, okay?"

"I'm listening."

"You are a brilliant and special boy. One day you will become one of the greatest men on Earth."

"I will? I am?"

"Yes you are, Steven. Now, step away from the cliff. Let me answer all the questions that are going on in your mind."

I did what Tiga said. He no longer felt like a strange

alien, but a guardian angel who showed up to steer me onto the right path.

"I want to apologize for saying that you are my experiment subject, Steven. I never knew that humans are such complicated and emotional creatures."

"It's okay. I'm sorry too for overreacting."

"In the past two days I have been wandering around Earth trying to find an answer to your question. Listen to me, Steven, every person on Earth exists for his own purpose. Have you ever wondered what the purpose of garbage men are? If there are no garbage men in your city, the trash will pile up. When the rain falls and water seeps into the ground, that trash will leak into the water and plants and destroy your environment.

"You see? All the world's a stage, and all the men and women merely players. They have their exits and their entrances; and one man in his time plays many parts. Everyone exists for a reason. Everyone exists for many reasons."

"Then what is my purpose?"

"You will become a great man, Steven. Your purpose is left for you to find."

"Ugh, you are only saying this to comfort me."

"No, Steven, I am telling the truth. I never lie."

"I just hope there is a time machine. Then I could do things differently."

"Like what?"

"I wouldn't confront Mr. Nevinson. I would do 100 pages of grammar practices everyday. They are right, I am Bobo. To them, I am only a stupid Communist who can't even speak their slang. At least I should improve my English before trying to earn their respect."

"Steven, I'm impressed that you learn so fast. I think my mission here is accomplished."

"Accomplished? So you are going to return to your planet?"

"I told you Steven, I don't have a planet. My existence is a continuum that consists of thousands of possibilities. Some are big, some are small; some I'm here, some I'm there. My spirit exists in forms of energy that do not follow the rules of space and time."

"So you are like a particle?"

"I am a particle. I am millions of particles. I know it's hard for you to understand, but you will one day when you become that great man. Technology is growing fast on Earth, and you will become part of the development. Remember my words, Steven."

"I will become a great man," I repeated to myself.

"Go back to your mother. She must be worried."

"Tiga, do you have a home?"

"I don't need a home."

"And you won't die either?"

"No, death is only a matter to humans. Steven, all the creations in the universe operate like a wheel. The end of infinity is zero, and the beginning of zero is infinity. Instead of visualizing your eventual demise, it is better to take it as a new starting point."

I felt the voice fading away again.

"Are you leaving me again, Tiga?" I squeaked.

"I don't belong here," Tiga replied, "I already said too much. One last thing, remember to grow; remember to learn; remember to do what will benefit society. One day you will be respected and thanked."

"No, no, no, don't go! I don't belong here either! I despise this planet. Everyone here kills to survive. And soon, the weak will become extinct. I've never felt loved by anyone on Earth. Nobody has cared for me the way you did. Take me with you, Tiga. Take my soul with you."

"Steven, it is not yet the time. You will become a great man on Earth. If one is different, one is bound to be lonely. One day you will understand the purpose of your existence. Go back home and go to sleep. When you open your eyes again, everything will turn back into the way you pleased."

"Please don't leave me, Tiga. You are my only friend."

"Goodbye, Steven. Don't feel alone. I am you. And I will always be there because you are always here."

"Don't go, please…"

The other me left as the sky lost its light.

And he never showed up again.

8

"Steven, Steven!"

I heard a scaly finger tapping impatiently on my desk. I peeled open my heavy eyelids and saw Mr. Nevinson standing in front of me, frowning.

"Are you giving up already on your participation marks?"

"Sorry, teacher." I sat up straight and saw that the classroom was half empty. "Is it already recess?" I thought to myself.

"Teacher, I am, am, sorry."
"Sorry? About what?"
"For making the class... emm... yesterday, noisy."
"Steven, you didn't make a sound. However, you should apologize for falling asleep in class."

I glanced around in a daze and grabbed my familiar

looking outfit in confusion.

"Teacher, what date is today?"
"Monday, Steven."

Monday?

My world turned upside down. I ran towards my locker, like a crazy ape who just escaped its lab. *Nothing.* There was absolutely nothing drawn on my locker. "The janitor must have already cleaned it up," I tried to convince myself.

"Steven?" Cindy walked towards me, "Did you finish your ESL homework? I'm kinda stuck on question 8."
"Cindy, what day is today?"
"Huh? Monday, why?"
"What *day* is it?"
"October 1st."
"Did anything happen to me yesterday? Or earlier today?"
"Are you okay? Your face is so red, looks like you have a high fever."
"Answer my fucking question!"
"Okay, Okay! Chillax, Bobo! No, I did not see you yesterday. How in the world should I know what happened to you? Oh Bobo you must be out of your mind."
"Yes I am out of my mind," I murmured.
"What?"
"Leave me alone!" I wrapped my arms around my head.

No, this was *not* possible.

When you open your eyes again, everything will turn back into the way you pleased.

So this was what he meant. I finally understood.

"Bobo, here! Come here!" The seniors called.

I gazed right into their eyes and straightened my back. I was shocked by my abnormal reaction. If the stereotype couldn't be overthrown, at least let me be a baboon with dignity and power. Not all prey have to be beasts. Not all prey are afraid of the hunters. I was a baboon with hair on every place except for my chest, which was where I kept my courage and my power. It was where I held my race, my nation, and my forgivingness.

With them, I was fearless.

I walked towards the seniors. With my hideous English, I stammered with all my might. "My name is Steven, Steven Sheng. My English is bad, but I am trying hard to learn. My country is weak, but it is doing its best to change. Let me repeat, I am Steven Sheng. And I am proud of my name. I am proud of my country."

"And one day," I promised myself, "I will prove it. I will prove it to you all."

9

For the past few years, I have told this story to many people on stage. Most treated me as a mad tech entrepreneur who made up these fancy stories to fool angel investors. Had I ever doubted in myself? Of course I had.

There was absolutely no proof. Even the book disappeared. The librarian told me that there was no such serial number. Because my English was so bad back then, I couldn't remember or understand the book's name.

But there was one thing that was certain: the pencil sketch. Sadly, I didn't have any photos of it. During my high school years, I tried writing many more questions on the desk, holding onto hope that I would receive a reply.

But he never returned.

As time passed by, my memories of my childhood in Texas became cloudier and cloudier. In the past 15 years, I took most of my time to reflect on myself and what I was capable of. My mama thought I was crazy because I suddenly became a straight-A student. My grades helped me enroll as a Physics major at MIT. Perhaps this happened because I never gave up my love and quest for knowledge and my search for answers to existential questions.

The deeper I dug into physics, more questions than answers came to me. This defeated my self confidence. I again began to see myself as others did: strange, weird, and shut-in. However in my third year, I discovered the field of quantum physics. I suddenly started to find answers to my questions and my mysterious childhood.

After I completed my bachelor's degree, many people had asked me to stay in America. "If you want to become a tech entrepreneur, you should go to Silicon Valley. There are more opportunities and resources there," they all said. But I refused. Many people thought that I had made the wrong decision, but I knew exactly what I was doing.

I need to prove to the world that what happened in my childhood was not a bizarre dream.

10

"Mr. Sheng, there is a guest waiting for you in the lobby. Should I send him up?"

"Do I have an appointment today?"

"Not that I know of, Mr. Sheng. He says he is an investor and would like to talk to you about your quantum mechanics project."

"Alright. Send him up then."

I heard three even knocks. A man with a black turtleneck and dark emerald suit showed up at my door.

"May I come in?" he asked with his coarse, deep voice.

"Of course. Please, have a seat. Would you like some coffee or tea?"

"I'm good, thanks."

"Great to meet you, sir," I eyed him curiously. "What may I call you?"

"Mr. He."

"It is a great pleasure meeting you, Mr. He. Thank you for coming over. My assistant told me that you are interested in my project proposal?"

"Yes. I am also interested in your story."

"You have heard about my story?"

"Your last pitch in Shenzhen. I was there."

"Oh, what a coincidence! How did you like it?"

"Quantum technology is the future. It will revolutionize the tech industry by eliminating the limits of space and time. In less than 50 years, quantum mechanics and quantum computing will be applicable to almost every aspect of our life."

"Yes, yes!" I burst out excitedly.

"But…"

Ugh, here it comes.

"But that is a fact that everyone already knows. It doesn't add any credibility to your project. And I would like to know, Steven, how are you planning to actually achieve time travelling? We all understand the concept, but achieving it sounds absurd if you can't use real technology or formulas to prove it."

"I don't want to lie to you, Mr. He, but the project is still in its experimental stage. However, the concept is coming along. I am confident that it will be accomplished within ten years."

"This still sounds science fiction to me. By the way, how is your funding coming along? Experiments like these needs billions of dollars."

I hesitated to tell him that if he was willing to invest in my project, he would be my first investor. My anxiety returned.

"This one may be another failure," I thought to myself. "Just like the hundreds of others."

"I think the project needs more credible advisors and scientists to back it up. If you think I'm qualified, I am here to help." Mr. He handed me a gold embossed emerald business card. "Contact me whenever you need, Steven. It was great meeting you."

"Mr. He?"
"Yes?"
"Do you believe in parallel universes? Do you believe that there is another self who exists in a higher dimension?"
"I don't know Steven. You are the one to find out. But I have an instinct that you will become a great man."

"That sounds familiar." I murmured.

"Excuse me?"
"Nothing. It's just that you reminded me of an old friend."
"Oh? Well, the future is whatever you choose to believe."
"The future is whatever you choose to believe." I repeated to myself.

"Goodbye, Steven."

"Steven, you will become a great man one day." The voice echoed in my head.
"I miss you, pal." I felt my eyes well up with hot tears.

"You are my only friend."

- FIN -

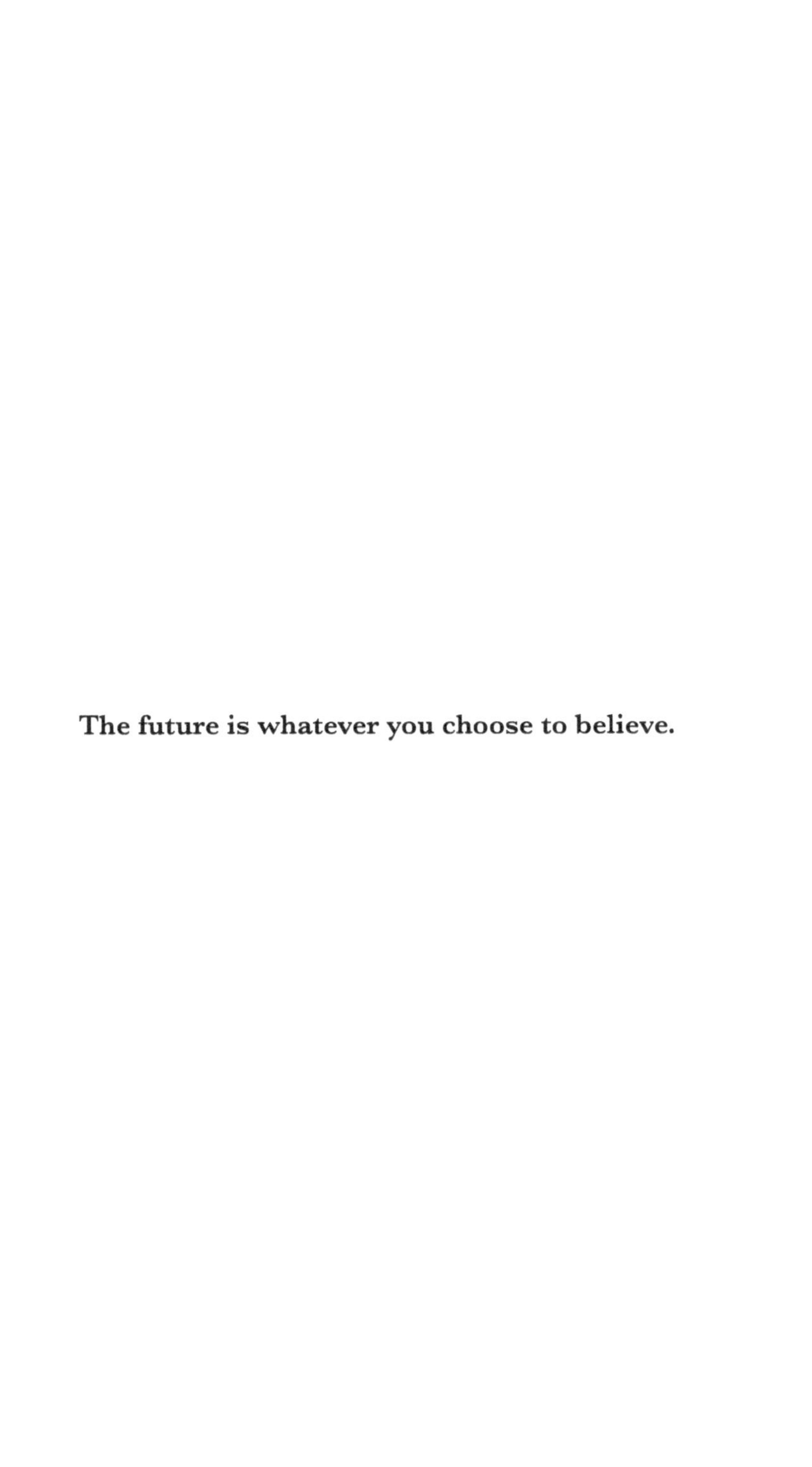

The future is whatever you choose to believe.

Connect with the Author

Film Producer, Writer, Entrepreneur

Bella D.

Instagram @imbe11a
lenstudioinc@gmail.com

www.lenstudioinc.com